Situations
Of
I

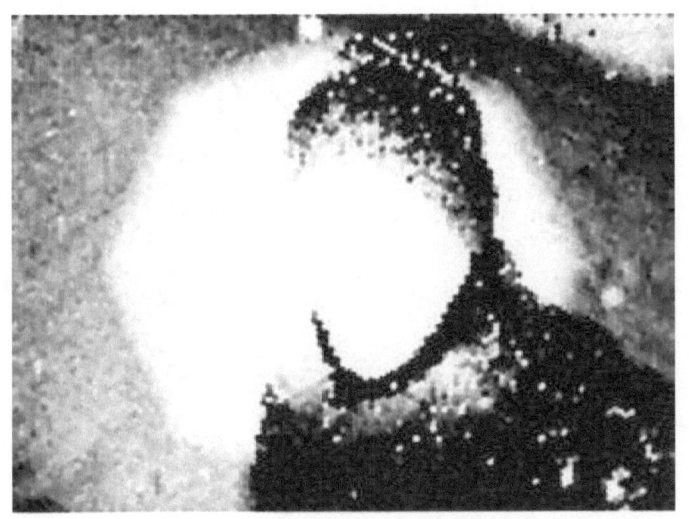

David W. Weimer

One and Only Press

Situations Of I

First Edition: 2015

Printed in the United States of America

Font: Estrangelo Edessa

Cover photographs and interior images produced by Andrée and David Weimer.

Main entry under title: Situations Of I

1. Magical Realism 2. Essays 3. Poetry 4. Short Stories

ISBN: 978-0-9850578-2-4

Visit the author's website:

www.oneandonlyobserver.wordpress.com

This is dedicated to the Muse, and to all manifestations of creation.

Preface

Flushing is a once-prosperous ridgeline rural village in the rolling hills of Belmont County, in northeastern Ohio, U.S.A. I tell those who have been here their whole lives, "I'm a transplant." They know. They can tell I'm not from here.

When asked where I'm from, I generally answer, "I grew up in Michigan." It's true. But it means almost as little to me as it does to the person I'm answering.

I'm used to my surroundings *here*, now, and I know my way around somewhat.

I've felt like this in other "hometowns"—in Pittsburgh; Memphis; Stuttgart, Germany; Ramonville Saint Agne, France; Howell and Fowlerville, Michigan; St. Clairsville, Ohio; Lake City, Florida; Moundsville, West Virginia; Fort Sill, Oklahoma; Fliegerhorst Kaserne, Germany and Cookeville, Tennessee.

I've celebrated Christmases and birthdays in each home; I've been sick, tired and happy in each of these places, too.

All of my homes have been comfortably mine. I've repaired things in them, vacuumed, dusted, done the dishes, cleaned the cat box, changed light bulbs, put folded laundry in drawers, left my shoes by the door, drank coffee, watched TV and listened to music there.

It's the familiar routines that do it for me, and tracing the same movement patterns each day.

I feel at home on Earth. I'm sure I could feel at home on another planet. There are many worlds of being here, just on this one. As many worlds as there are places to live.

I don't think my string of hometowns will end in Flushing. Normandy, France would be nice.

Situations Of I is a collection of vignettes, essays, philosophic musing and poetry that I assembled in *this* place; this place is always where I am, where I'm living. I've used the tools and materials at hand.

Welcome.

Introduction

The *Muse*....

I'm striving to become as much a servant to it as possible; to get out of the way, in other words. The more I do that, the more often things go smoothly and... strangely. When I'm trying to pull the reins and control the direction, it's always a struggle. I've learned to trust the horse to find its way. I've learned to not worry about the placement of its feet as we fly over blurring terrain. The horse doesn't need me to tell it how to run like a horse.

Each piece in this collection is centered on the unique free-floating magical reality I take completely for granted—my individual awareness.

Situations wrote itself. I hugged the horse's neck in the dark, reins held loosely; the black stallion with the blaze on his forehead flattened his ears, leaned forward and surged over fields, hooves drumming the blurring earth and throwing clods of grass and soil into the air behind us.

Distinctions blur with such freedom. An essay is something else and a story isn't what it seems. A poem becomes a story and a story acts like a poem. None of it is fiction, and all of it is "made up."

In the following pages you will find yourself standing at the edge of my pond. A wind is moving the trees over there and a fish just jumped to accompany the distant growling buzz of a chainsaw.

In other words: *Now.*

Table of Contents

Chapter 1 — Does My Dog Like My Music?

I say that music is reality; as real as my tabletop. *Okay, stinging hand*: feel the burn in my palm—I hear the song and hit the table again—*Real*.

Songs are complete universes and I get lost in them each time.

A performer grows older, or dies, and I still have their song, perfectly preserved, just like he and I *used* to be. Like we always have been.

My feelings are carried higher, soaring above long-ago reawakened days. Each time I listen I remember.

Again.

Always just like this.

Again.

Only more so.

I always feel what I remember when my song plays. Every time, and then I remember it more. Like *this.*

What would a world of silence *be*? Could it be nostalgia? Could it grow in me like a volume-less speaker?

Nothing.

No thing.

With just silence, I'd hear my silence (but I wouldn't *know* that's what it was) looping over and over again. Silence would be my song.

From songs to me.

From too quiet, to too loud to stand.

Can't I keep my songs when I go away forever? Maybe there's music *made* of me. Could I *be* silence? Something tells me, "Yes, I will be; one day."

For now—for right now—push 'play' on that God-blessed cassette player, CD player and iPhone. Turn on that turntable. Set the needle gently down in the outer groove. Gently.

And keep them ALL playing. Thank God. Thank God. Keep them *all* playing.

Does my dog, Mike, like my music? Maybe he can't hear it.

Maybe he's listening to something I can't hear.

Chapter 2 — Home is Where I Live

I live in a village in northwestern Belmont County in Eastern Ohio. I've lived in Michigan, Florida, Pennsylvania, West Virginia, Tennessee and Ohio and in three countries: the U.S., Germany and France. Now I'm here.

I've settled down here with my family in the "Ohio Valley," an area comprising parts of the northwest West Virginia panhandle, Southwestern Pennsylvania and Northeastern Ohio.

Flushing was a more thriving and vibrant place in the 1800s through the first half of the 1900s. From its beginning, on November 9th, 1813, when Jesse Foulke drew the first plat and named this place, until today, my present home village has seen much change. Former prosperity is evident in the old downtown buildings and evinced in the period photos on display at *Shutway Hardware*, in *Carpenter's Pizzeria* and in the *Underground Railroad Museum* downtown. Most of the businesses that used to thrive here have closed. My current home village celebrated its 200th birthday recently.

Quakers originally settled this place, building a school, a hospital, stores, restaurants, other businesses and many, many homes. From 1825 to 1895 they were a major presence. Now, right across the street from my house, the "Friend's Cemetery" is nearly the only remaining obvious landmark. My older son and I throw a football along the grass in front of it because our yard is small and a cherry tree blocks high trajectory throws. I see visitors stopping across the street occasionally, quietly looking for specific graves. The same couple mows it every two weeks or so in the summer. They're probably Quakers. In town, The Quaker Meeting House on High Street burned down in 1959 after being empty for years. I don't know what happened to the Quaker majority here. Maybe they're here, still. Some of the old families are still here, I've been told.

Until World War I, nearly all of the coal mining in this area was underground. Flushing was right in the middle of it. The coal is close to the surface. Flushing and the surrounding farmland are made from coal. The Cleveland, Lorain and Wheeling Railway entrance into the southwest end of town let the small mines that dotted this area become viable commercial ventures because the railway shipped their coal away through Holloway and west, on to

Cambridge. Railroad tracks used to wind their way through this area, hauling uncounted tons of the fossilized black organic matter to furnaces and steel mills. The train tunnel still exists in town, mostly undamaged but abandoned. Recently, strip mining was expanded north and south of us—within eyesight—and more recently—precisely this moment—the big, big boom of drilling for gas and the gangbusters hydraulic fracturing, "fracking," for this gas and oil is exploding all around us; we're right in the middle of the frying pan.

By the mid-1900s coal mining had tapered off in this vicinity because the coal here is typically high in sulfur, which had become less desirable. The market, however, for this coal has recently grown again—due to a more sophisticated processing, overseas buying and new coal refining uses. As a result, coal mining here has picked back up, both underground and surface mining.

The hills here are shaved and honeycombed. Uncountable straws are sucking gas and oil from under us and the newly-laid turquoise pipelines are taking it away. Much of the open terrain around here is comprised of active and reclaimed surface "strip" mines. As a result, the beautiful views along these ridges of rolling hills of grass are tree-free.

Beginning in 1959, forty years of educating the local region's children added to Flushing's former prosperity. A regional school was established and housed within the grand four-story structure and a couple of outbuildings on the high ground at the west end of town. Proud parents shopped in the numerous stores here. There were several gas stations. The area's children joined baseball and football teams, competing on the village's nearby sports fields.

In 1998, a new Union Local district school was completed near Morristown, eight miles south from here, and the kids and their parents—such a permanent-seeming fixture for so long—were gone.

Today, the Flushing elementary school building sits empty, windows boarded up or broken, with two spreading breeches in the upside-down hull of the imposing roof, growing on either side of a once-proud bell tower. The building is filled, I've heard, with asbestos and Flushing doesn't have the money or the will to renovate or remove the structure. I've also heard that there's no asbestos. Maybe they're waiting for State or Federal cleanup funds. In any case, empty swing set frames and a now silent, sloping grass lawn border the grounds.

The former *Cloverland Dairy* is located one block south, perpendicular to High Street. This large, formerly-prosperous dairy rests, deserted, its loading docks abandoned, a hundred yards behind the Flushing Christian Church, one of four surviving, formerly more active, churches downtown. The Flushing Senior Center is in the lower level at the rear of this church. I built an awning for over the door and replaced a couple of toilets in the women's room there. I also built a wooden alter for the chapel in the front of the building and re-glazed and repainted the large windows in the front and along side.

In the back of the church, standing outside of the senior center door, you can see the dairy now because the large sheet metal building between the two places has recently collapsed.

On the southern edge of town, along Route 149, just outside the village limits, is *Hillandale Farms*, a consolidated egg supplier for local Walmart, Riesbeck's and Kroger stores. It's pretty busy. I don't know where the chicken farms are, but *Hillandale* sells a lot of eggs.

After the subsurface coal mining petered out here, the train tracks that once guided trains through the village were removed. When the school was moved, parents and their kids quit coming here. A community clock in front of the Flushing Municipal Building had stood, broken, for years. Just this winter it was replaced by a digital time-and-temperature unit.

Today, the demographic of Flushing is largely older, although there *are* families with children here. For eight years, between my bread-and-butter painting and handyman contracts, I did a fair amount of handyman and maintenance work for the retired senior citizens and widows in the village.

Many houses, unrepaired, are now broken down or empty. Last winter, on a slow news day for WTOV channel 9, a camera crew came here for the evening news when a front porch, as well as part of the roof, collapsed on a 90-year-old man's dilapidated home—and the elderly gentleman refused to leave. After a brief standoff with firefighters, police and EMT personnel, the man was eventually removed and his house demolished.

Flushing is still alive, like the peach tree around a deadwood center is still alive. There *are* still families dotted through the village whose young children attend the Head Start preschool on the bottom floor of a large brick building at the west end of town. Not many, but definitely not none. The combination

Convenient general store and *Marathon* gas station are still open every day. This is the only place "downtown" now for groceries. It turns a decent profit selling fried chicken lunches and dinners to locals, miners and gas workers. It runs a deli, sells pizza and rents DVDs. The prices are higher than we like, but what are you going to do? The next comparable grocery store is ten miles away, in Morristown or in New Athens. Walmart, Kroger and Riesbeck's are in St. Clairsville, fifteen miles away. *Convenient*, owned by a German woman living near Morristown, is conveniently here.

Carpenter's Pizzeria satisfies those of us looking for quick hot food. *Shutway Hardware* is open six days a week and occasionally saves me the 23-mile round-trip to *Lowe's Home Improvement* in the strip mall past St. Clairsville off I-70.

Country Carryout sits a few hundred yards past the east end of Flushing, the "CCO." It runs a brisk business selling beer, cigarettes and lottery tickets to miners, gas workers and locals from all the area villages driving by on Route 331. I go there myself to buy inexpensive *Carlo Rossi* merlot; Flushing is a "dry" town and this is the closest place. Irene, its owner, is at the helm most of the time I stop in. "Some of the best years of my life," she said, eyes alight, "were spent there."

We were talking about the now-closed *New Co-Op* grocery store on this end of town, but still within the village limits. The large former grocery store building now houses *Hornswogglers Market—Buy, Sell, Trade*. This is its most recent incarnation after a number of years of various start-ups and dormant periods. Irene told me that she went there this winter, back to the refrigerated display she used to stock with cut meat. There's a flea market in that part of the building now. Standing there, she started crying. She said it was because of all the memories the rusted display unit opened up.

Her store, the CCO, which she's been running for twenty-seven years, catches traffic through Flushing as well as that heading to or coming from New Athens and Cadiz; there's an intersection a stone's throw away where the road going there starts. The road going north to Cadiz is downhill and winding; it feels like it's going south. There's a big strip mine between New Athens and Cadiz, and a big pipeline construction supply depot. There's also a big gas compressor plant on the way there. It's stunning, every time I drive by on my way to Pittsburgh, to see so much turquoise green gas pipeline stacked in one area. And flames, and towers and storage tanks. There's an old bowling alley in New Athens that we go to once or twice a year, usually during church pizza nights. This year, my younger son's birthday party was there.

We lost our village post office in 2012 due to federal United States Postal Service cutbacks. In 2013 *Peoples Bank*, our bank, closed its Flushing branch and we had to move our accounts next door, to WesBanco.

Directly opposite the old Methodist Church (which is right next door to our "new" bank), the *Victoria Read Public Library*, a center for studious children and local families, had to reduce its hours to a few hours a day, four days a week—a fraction of what it once offered patrons. A recently increased millage property tax is letting them expand their hours again. I built some shelves, did some soffit repair work and replaced a toilet in the men's room at the library. Our village diner burned down in 2012.

Several chisel-marked sandstone blocks now form the walls of a play area in our back yard near my boys' swing set and clubhouse. Similar blocks form an arc in front of a campfire ring at the base of a hillside closer to my house. All of these formed foundation stones are from a church and school that stood a hundred years ago today on the other side of our too-narrow main street, next to Friend's Cemetery. Those two structures used to stand proudly next to that little cemetery. The cemetery is all that remains. A forty-year-old mobile home trailer sits where the church bell once rang, and next to that, another, twin, trailer is crumbling to pieces while a Vietnam veteran lives in it without running water, I understand. They recently disconnected his gas. Another pile of sandstone foundation blocks sits in the steep grade lot next to one of Missy Smith's rental houses on the left side of Main Street, going into town—this was the Quaker's hospital building. The Underground Railroad Museum downtown has a picture of this former hospital in a display case on the front of the building.

Yes, Flushing is still alive, yes. It *has* seen busier, different, younger days. The grass is still cut regularly by village employees in the park where I like to go. The streets are snowplowed in the winter. In 2010, High Street, our main street, was repaved. This was because of the gasland boom which came shortly afterward, and the need for good, solid roads to transport drilling and gas line heavy equipment. Until then, our narrow roadway had been in very bad shape. The roads leading to Flushing have been widened slightly.

The winter of 2012-2013 was a mild one, luckily, for the company contracted to replace all of our village's water supply lines. They were installed in 1939.

There are "strip-mining" surface coal mines on the north and south edges of town. Twenty-four hours a day, the sounds of machinery and beeping as huge construction vehicles back up are alternately loud and faint, depending on the wind. Now, newly-drilled petroleum gas wells glow on the underside of clouds at night like massive jack-o'-lanterns whenever a well taps into the petroleum seam.

Twenty-four miles east of us and several hundred feel lower in elevation than Flushing, the Ohio River runs from Pittsburgh in the north through Wheeling, West Virginia, on its northeast to southwest track. I am in Wheeling each Tuesday night for a philosophy meeting at the Ohio County Public Library. I also "scout" for books there at local thrift stores; I'm a bookseller.

I'm home.

It's February 2012 [I wrote eight months ago, and ago, and ago and ago].

For eight years, I have been a contractor handyman painter. Last year's weather helped me resolve to do something different for a livelihood. My outdoor painting season typically begins in the second or third week of May, once the average outside temperature, day and night, is around fifty degrees Fahrenheit, just when the spring rains have given way to longer, clearer, lengthening days.

But last May, this never happened. The rains didn't stop. I had a line of scheduled outside painting jobs marked on my calendar and I told my customers, "It looks like we're rained out this week, so we'll reschedule for *next* week..." Living hand-to-mouth as a contractor, several weeks of postponed work with no steady income gets my serious attention.

Hoping against hope, I worked inside jobs, always with my eyes turned skyward, watching those clouds, waiting for a break in the rains that never came. I limped along for the rest of May into June. I had been loathe to give up my outdoor painting, because this was my bread-and-butter, as well as the income that allowed me to survive my annual slow-down around Christmas until after New Year's.

Ah, 2011. The year of the rain. I have to thank it.

In 2010, in January and February, I had taken a hiatus from contracting in order to work on my first book, *Portrait of a Seeker: Born to Wonder.*

I had become determined to break into writing as a full-time occupation. The summer before, 2009, I had injured my "good" knee, and had worked—hanging drywall ceilings, painting baseboard trim on my knees on the floor, and carrying railroad ties and bricks for landscape steps and patios—all while hobbling on a knee that hurt with each step.

So I took a break from handyman work during my winter slow-down to work on the book that I'd begun six years earlier upon first returning to the U.S. from living abroad. We were in Michigan then. After a brief beginning, the unfinished book sat untouched, collecting dust, as the years flowed on by, on by.

Since those back-to-back years of pain and then rain, I have published *Portrait of a Seeker,* as well as two other books, *A Handyman's Common Sense Guide to Spiritual Seeking* and *Ben and the Dragon*.

This is my fourth. Fortunately, I'm spending more of my time writing than handymaning.

But... going back to that January in 2010. It was my first step onto the road of being a writer and the beginning of working to make my first book a reality. I had the desperation born of watching a lot of years go on by. It was frigid and snowing.

We had more than two feet of snow that January and February. Because I was not working physically, I had decided to exercise each day—push-ups, sit-ups and walking. For the walking, I would drive to Shuler Park on the edge of town where there is a pond. I would park my GMC work van on the ridge lane that overlooks baseball fields and a fenced-in tennis court along the wood line. I'd stomp downhill, across the fields, then cut into the woods and hike down another steep, tree-filled area to the evergreen-encircled pond, where the village Ruritan club holds an annual spring fishing tournament. It was frozen and snow-covered.

In the first month of the year, in the dead of winter, I would stomp through the drifting snow to stand among the ring of trees as the wind pushed at me and as the swirling snow collected on my eyelashes. The sound of wind through the needles of the evergreens, and, blowing itself through the deciduous trees beyond the pond, was a thinly-modulating noise of timelessness, basic survival, forgotten warmth and frozen-solid nights.

I would stand for ten minutes doing nothing, thinking nothing. I had an objective. These ten minutes. This time, right now. *This.*

I would stand and become my awareness in this present time. And then, I would turn and booted feet would take a first step away, and then other step would follow each other repeatedly around the edge of the pond, past the covered picnic shelter, uphill to a snow-covered oval path that circles a cleared slope where two swing sets, a set of silver-painted monkey bars, a long stainless steel slide, a red merry-go-round and a yellow fiberglass spiral slide all wait silently for children.

I'd step through calf- and knee-high snow, and circle this sloped football field-sized area four or five times. First uphill, paralleling a treed fence line bordering a field, and then, upon summiting the oval park beneath giant, leafless Sycamore branches, I would overlook the secluded valley while walking slowly, catching my breath, before curving once more downhill, angling to the right as the way becomes level when I near the first metal swing set.

I'd then hike off the path to the monkey bars, do five pull-ups, and stomp back through the deep snow to my line of tracks, curving right, to begin my uphill ascent again, walking in my own evenly-spaced tracks, stepping into snow-filling holes, leaving others behind.

On this day that I'm remembering, in January of 2010, I wear snow pants, snow boots, a blue knit scarf, a heavy snowboarding coat, insulated gloves and a knit hat.

My boys were in their perfect snow sledding prime, eight and eleven, and our family was accustomed to coming to this park—although on the other side of the high ridge, below another playground made of wood standing on a hilltop.

When school was cancelled during the snow season, it had become an almost daily routine.

We snowboard now, and have different plastic sleds to replace those that are broken. The boys are older and there are ever-changing things they want to try.

"*Short Story 1*," is the first story in this collection centering on my life in Flushing. It takes place, appropriately, in this meditative winter walking park.

Following that first winter slow-down beginning, I returned to contracting work after a few weeks when I had to spend a large chunk of our winter savings to rebuild the transmission in my wife's Pontiac Montana. The rest of that year went fine, contracting work-wise. Jobs came in. I made money. The following year was that rainy one I talked about.

"Rainy two thousand eleven" was an insistent wake up call: get a job not dependent on the weather.

After five months of rain, the opportunity arose in south central New York State to spend much of the summer working on a horse farm owned by a fellow member of a philosophic organization, the TAT Foundation. At our April TAT meeting, Nina told me, "You should bring your family and spend the summer on my farm." She had a lot of work that needed to be done which had gone unattended during her husband's long illness and eventual death.

I took Nina up on her offer. If I'd been involved in my usual outdoor painting projects, I wouldn't have gone. On Windy Hill Farm, near Binghamton, NY, I repaired fences, fixed gutters on barns, built a deck on the back of Nina's house, re-hung her house's gutters and de-algae-d her roof—as well as a myriad of other handyman-type repair and improvement projects. It wasn't raining in this part of New York like it was in Flushing.

When we returned to Flushing in August, I mowed our hayfield back yard, lined up some inside contracting work and finished out the year with two projects: building a deck for a woman in Wheeling, and insulating a basement and renovating the small bathroom for a widow living east of St. Clairsville, Ohio. These would be my last contracting jobs. All during the summer in New York and upon returning, I was writing and editing *Portrait of a Seeker* before work and in the evenings.

In 2011, the year of rain, I resisted accepting any outside work that required multiple dry days or weeks. People wanted me to work like that but I knew that the rain would kill me, livelihood-wise.

A moment-in-time is etched into my memory: bending over, attempting to keep the rain off my electric drill by sheltering it with my body as I drive 3-inch coated deck screws through decking boards and into floor joists with water dripping constantly from my nose.

Water dripped from the bill of my painter's baseball hat and also ran off the edge of my raincoat, soaking my lower back.

I (belatedly) remembered to put my wallet inside my lunchbox to keep it dry from the rain; it had become half-soaked already. In the van at lunch, with the heater running, I spread the wallet's soggy contents over the wide heater vent of the dash in my GMC work van. Bills, business cards and receipts stuck, drying in a drooped shape, later that day while

I drove home in the dark under constantly-moving windshield wipers.

A determination was blazing with heat inside of me: *Never this again*.

Rain is no big deal, but I'd watched myself struggling to meet bills and answer the inevitable car repairs along with other always unforeseen home-related expenses this past year; I was determined to do something that *wasn't so damned reliant* on dry weather.

My tool belt hangs in my workroom in the basement now—except when I'm working around the house. Whenever I see it, I'm a little sad. It used to be my constant companion traveling on the passenger seat next to me like a faithful dog.

I use this keyboard now. My tool belt only gets to go with me now when I do something around the house or for a friend. It came out of retirement briefly, two days ago, when I repaired a kitchen faucet for a former customer and then trimmed some tree branches over another friend's roof.

Trimming those branches, pushing my 32-foot Werner aluminum extension ladder up under the soffit at the corner of Beth's second floor home, I experienced nostalgia for the livelihood I used to have, re-appreciating the skills I had developed in something as simple-sounding as moving ladders around. Simultaneously, I re-experienced a strengthening resolve to by-God succeed as a writer.

Today [I wrote ago, and ago and ago], I will go to the pond in Flushing Park. It's been a mild winter so far, with far more rain than snow and the temperature remaining above freezing.

Yesterday morning, however, and throughout the day, it snowed. We have three inches on the ground. The boys came home from school and Andrée and I went sledding with them at the park. We had a blast. Andrée, Benjamin, Guillaume, Mike (our adopted English Labrador) and I romped in the new white stuff until dark. It was fun and, most certainly, exercise hiking up that long, long hill.

This morning, I'm looking forward to putting my boots on and driving down to the ridge road where I'll park and walk downhill, then across the snow-covered ball fields and down another narrow path through the woods to the pond's edge.

Bright light flows from the windows behind me as I type at my corner desk.

"This is the feeling of a first winter of hope," I write. I don't know what it means, but I know exactly what it means.

I'm looking forward to standing at the pond, breathing the cold air and listening. Being.

Now I'm at the pond.

This sure beats working.

When I'm working, I'm completely engaged and don't look up, or pause or stop.

The first time I stood here at the pond, a year ago in January, I was astonished and surprised:

> "Oh my God. *It has been so long....*
> *I used to live here, in this magical*
> *place of stillness and noticing things*
> *and wonder. I used to **be** here all of the*
> *time, steeped in wonder and mystery—*
> *where everything is new and all of my*
> *life is ahead of me and there is the*

*promise of...everything.... I haven't
been here for so long...."*

I was grateful and scared. I had been allowed to return to this beauty, openness and wonder after sleeping to these things for thirty-plus years. And my sons *still* live here.... *Still.* I used to, too.

I am deeply moved to discover that this place still exists for me. I hope I never do anything to mess it up for my boys. I probably will, but I hope not.

"Thank you," I told the pond that
first time standing there.

I said those words to the pond, eyes stinging, two years ago (and ago and ago), while standing in the snow. I haven't been back to the pond many times this winter. I've been busy. Today is the first day of spring and I look out the back window and see impossibly large snowflakes falling like dandelion feathers, covering everything. This is where I live.

Chapter 3 — *Run*

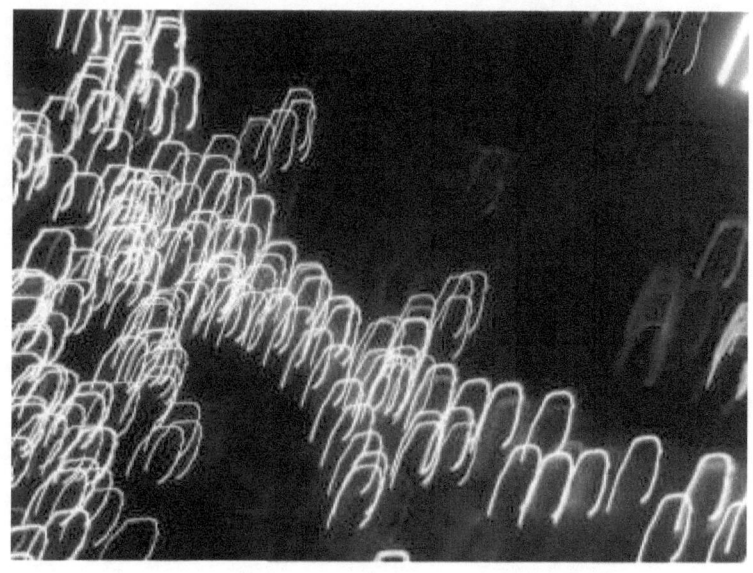

Running?

Sure. There's a time for that. And you do that until it's not the thing anymore. And when you're tired of running—or when you have to (this is always the same thing)—you stop.

And fighting isn't so bad, even when it's bad. Even when something is damaged. It's not as bad as the anticipatory fear you'd been running from before you stop and finally get to work. Nothing's as bad as the fear of anticipation.

Why can't we be born into a world where we can run free without worries or fear? Why do we have to constantly kill, consume and be killed? We're being killed now, from the inside and outside.

Who set up this whole arrangement? Why do we need to eat each other, we living—as opposed to dead—creatures? In *this* universe, it's inevitable. Why can't we just *be*? I guess even the sun destroys something every millisecond to be. Why was I brought here? We don't listen to the chickens and cows that ask that; we eat them.

I've had a lifelong love-to-hate relationship with my fellow species members. I get along better with the members of other species. It just feels like that. I don't have much in common with my dog, but we get along better with each other than we do with members of our own kind. There's no threat. Or maybe it's because we don't expect the other to understand us; we just accept them.

As members of the same species, you and I are fighting this damned eternal fight to keep up with what everyone else seems to be doing; caring what others say or think about us; fearing what others will do to us; judging others. *What if God was one of us?* This is a pop song title that no one asks because why would God want to do that (ask)?

What if God was *all* of us? Are all of my cells worshiping me? Or are they becoming atheists? What if God was none of us?

Abuser, abused; hater, hatee; bully, bullied; envier and envied.

Can't I list positive qualities? They exist, don't they? There are good people, aren't there?

Yes.

What makes a good person "good"? Why does anyone do anything, either good *or* bad? Positive or negative? Who is labeling these items good or positive? I think we do what we *are*, and there's not a lot of choosing going on.

Why does a man stay to the end of his shift, with no witnesses, finishing that damn job to the end, painting the tops of boards and surfaces that no one will ever see? Is he perfect? Or is he paranoid about being judged by some unseen future top-of-door-trim inspector?

Why does a man say, "To hell with it," and leave things undone and unfinished? Who is freer?

Why does a mother love her young? Why does a boy give part of his lunch to a hungry classmate? Do all children *want* to hug their parents or do they just do it? What does "want" mean? Are any of these things "good"? What *is* good? Good feels different from what I think of as bad, hateful and evil. But, when I'm angry, when I'm really mad at someone, I feel *right*.

Why are we this way? Is it all about survival? I think it is. Birds are born with instincts to do what *they* do. Are we any different? Not at all. We're born to do <u>exactly</u> what we do because our lineage has survived doing exactly that. The ones who did something else didn't make it.

Some of us embody warring opposites. *Some* of us? Try all. Some of us give in quickly to one side, allowing this side—usually communally accepted as "bad"—to rise to the surface. These are the people who do terrible things to another—not just thinking about doing them. Often individuals feel an urge to act violently toward another. A minority of us acts on these urges. Why?

And who in their right mind *wouldn't* want to leave all of this behind? To leave a place where such badness can be? Aren't there truly *good* human animals? Sure. Aren't there human animals that do harmful acts to other human animals? We're repeating ourselves here. Beyond doubt. IS "good" really good? Or is "good" a failure to act? I've heard it said that the killer is a free man. Well, he's killed. And someone else is dead, for now.

Are there human animals that are <u>not</u> unbalanced and hopelessly screwed up? Probably a few. By "screwed up" I mean unsteady in one's actions.

Show me a parent who *isn't* passing along to their children nearly all of their own hang-ups and failings (and surprisingly few of their very "positive" aspects), and I'll show you their spouse, who's doing exactly the same thing.

WHAT ABOUT:

Eventually he simply refused to deal with his fellow humans. This act was a step beyond his reaction of condemning his own kind for their reprehensible behavior.

He no longer remained fixed in his righteous indignation; he simply shut all of it out—all of the good, the bad, the right, the wrong—his interpretations of his fellow human's actions. He was finished.

Was he lonely? Oh, lonely. Oh, yes. Maybe there was someone who could relate to him. He knew that was possible. But it was simply better to not look.

He no longer ran from his own kind; he just stayed away.

"Hey! Hey buddy!"

This was always yelled at him. "They" were vacuums—they just couldn't stand to be ignored.

He didn't bother to ignore them any longer; he never turned their way. His head stayed down. He kept walking. The world was big enough; there was somewhere else. Always somewhere to move to.

One day, he would need something that he couldn't provide for himself. He would need help from his fellow humans. When that day comes, it would be the end of him—one way or another. He would then let go of his banishment and fall back into humanhood, or he would die a real death, unhelped, and perhaps alone.

Sometimes he was permitted a span of connected moments that felt like everything was as it was, as it should be. Perfect.

Chapter 4 — Another Run

[Février]

I ran everywhere when I was a child. As an 18- to 20-year-old, I ran daily in the Army—in the mornings for PT (physical training) and a few times a year for our regular PT test 2-mile runs. I ran daily for exercise, to counteract the fat-storing effect of drinking German beer. I was vain and appearance-conscious—unlike now....

In my late 20's and early 30's, I inline skated hundreds of miles on roads, sidewalks and parking lots in Pittsburgh, Wheeling and Memphis. Then I discovered skate parks and ramps in Stuttgart,

Germany, Southern France and later, back in the U.S.

During my late 30's, I began using my Nordic Track ski machine, the one that my first, practice, wife had given me for my birthday moments before telling me that she wanted a divorce. I kept the machine and took it with me wherever I moved because it seemed so potentially useful.

After that, for several years, until my mid-40's, I didn't do much running or skating or skiing.

Instead, I plodded along under loads of lumber, sheets of drywall, bags of concrete, sectioned railroad ties, old bathtubs, cans of paint, buckets of drywall mud, replacement toilets, rolls of tar paper, bundles of shingles and extension ladders. My steps were heavy and just as carefully-placed as an elephant or very large human walking on ice.

If my feet happened to slip while I was carrying something from one place to another on a job site or to my work van, I would go down like a slow motion sequoia, usually ending up sitting or kneeling with the load still in my arms or on my shoulder. For eight years, I walked, thus burdened, as a self-employed one-man-band, jack-of-all-trades handyman painter contractor.

On the last year of my handyman run, while watching my older son playing soccer for his third year from the sidelines in my folding chair, I shouted, "Don't give up! Come on, Gui! Go after the ball!" It was a matter of conditioning, I turned to my wife and explained; they need to keep running so that they'll be *able* to run.

On the last day of soccer, Gui's coach arranged for our team's parents to play against their kids. After five minutes in a forward position—or maybe sooner—I vowed to myself to never again urge Gui to run faster during a game. I ran and ran and hopelessly attempted to catch my breath. I never did catch it. I was out of breath for that entire interminable match. I ran, and panted, hands folded on top of my head whenever we had a blessed five-second break. I can still taste that iron flavor from my scorched lungs.

Not long ago, I was walking down a former railroad corridor on an asphalt walking path that parallels the Ohio River in Wheeling. It was for exercise; I wasn't working physically for a living anymore.

I had stepped off my slowly-moving contractor work train. I felt I was getting out of shape. I had been walking, strangely unbalanced without my tool belt's weight, without the familiar hammer handle thumping on the back of my leg with each step. My hammer hangs in my basement work room, unmoving.

On the trail, as I passed under the 19th century Wheeling Island suspension bridge with its see-through metal grate decking that allowed you to look up and see the vehicle undercarriages through it, I saw a few hundred yards ahead of me the boathouse of the Wheeling Yacht Club on the left side of the trail, the river side.

Run, something said.

Perhaps my silent companion who is always right and who never sleeps was trying to tell me something. My other hemisphere. My right mind. Maybe it was a whisper from a younger me, trapped inside of a soundproof box.

I experienced worrying thoughts of hurting my feet or knees or getting shin splints from such unaccustomed running.

The word repeated.

Run.

Excuses ignored, I began.

I began jogging carefully and lightly, and it occurred to me that people, and me, too, grow older and grow away from a very simple thought: the willingness and memory of running. Everyone formerly ambulatory *has* run before. Everyone formerly ambulatory—no matter how bad they look now, limping or rolling along.

The image of a carefully-walking old woman came to mind as I jogged. *Yes...* that definitely could be me. I *could* forget. *Could? How about, "do"... and "did."*

The concept of running becomes more and more a monumental-felt thing.

Run? Me? No. No. Of course not. When I was a child, sure, but not now....

How a word, "impossible," starts to attach, moss-like, to that short word, "run." Some probably couldn't run now to save their lives. Not *now*. And even if they could, they probably wouldn't let themselves try. They'd be too afraid of breaking something or of falling. I can see this in myself. They wouldn't run to save their lives because they'd be trying to save their lives by not running. This three-letter gun held to their heads, trigger pulled back—*Run*—would be met by the sobbing heartfelt words, "I **can't**."

Blam!

It's easy to envision such a scenario... in others. I prefer to think I would be different. But if I were 90? Would I dare to run? If I *could* run at 90, would running start my odometer turning backwards?

I'm going to walk again on the trail today. It's probably going to be raining down there in the Wheeling Ohio River valley. Up here, in Flushing, sleet and granular snow falls now, whispering on the grass. Today I'm going to run. Who knows what will come between me and this word, but I *will* it to happen.

After jogging that first time a combined six hundred yards from the bridge and back, I stopped and touched my toes, gently. I slowly stood straight again. I then walked to Heritage Port where my car was parked. My heart was pumping, my blood was moving. It felt good to be alive.

Yesterday, a gorgeous February sun shone in a clear blue sky over leafless trees and green-brown grass. The light struck the Wheeling Park playground. In a pond nearby, Mallard ducks paddled around. On a hillside opposite the park, thousands of headstones stood upright in the bright sunlight, guarding their buried namesakes.

My wife and I were sitting on a wooden bench, warmed by the sun. We watched our sons and their friends playing hide-and-seek and freeze tag. They were running everywhere. Walking only happened, briefly, between bursts of running.

"Ben!" a boy shouted from the swings.

My eight-year-old ran over to take the swing next to Noah, his friend from a nearby village who we'd brought along to the park.

I said to Andrée, "They run everywhere."

Each generation watches the younger one running up from behind to snatch a held-out baton in order to continue without stopping, without looking back....

Today, after lunch, I'm going to take my wife's car to drive to the post office in Holloway to mail my packaged books. Then I'll drive down to the river valley for my "local route" of visiting thrift stores and libraries looking for books to add to my shelves at home; I sell books. And write. I don't handyman work anymore.

Afterwards, a couple hours before tonight's *M&M Philosophy* meeting in Wheeling, I'll park somewhere along Water Street and walk down the concrete steps to Heritage Port and stop at the water's edge. After a while I'll go up some different steps to the paved path, and just beyond the playground shaped like a ship, just before I pass under the suspension bridge, I'll push off with one foot, and begin jogging.

Maybe I'll run a little harder this time.

Chapter 5 — Story #4, "An Uncharted Wreck"

[mai deux mille douze]

A dark front was moving in, in an ominous arc, looming above the soccer fields. A cooler breeze blows on the back of my head as I write.

A soccer game is what I'm here for. I thought I could get some writing done at the same time. Ten- and 12-year-olds are playing over there—red and black jerseys. Looking up to watch the game; looking back down to the paper. It's half time now. I've been looking up too much to connect these separated thoughts. I think I'll give up the scribbling of thoughts for now.

The sun shines hotly from under a scud of swift clouds.

Now, I'm simply staring at the sun. It's just come out from under that fast-moving dark cloud.

This star we call ours is high in the center of those clouds. Regal rays stream outward like a crown from a central region of brightness in the haze overhead.

The rest of this story re-submerges, under the depths of vagueness. Free, free, free from the confines of description and from the bonding chains of further words. This Not-Really-a-Thing remains undiminished in its timeless majesty. Floating, weightlessly, without discrimination, limits or observation.

This must sometimes be.

Chapter 6 — The Writer, or The Gazebo

[mai]

Stately fir, oak and maple trees stand guard in this pleasant-feeling glade. A high-ceilinged, gable-roofed, mostly single-level library rests on the hillside opposite from this background-wooded gazebo.

Ants, toiling inside their nests beneath volcano-shaped mounds centered over cracks in the mortar adjoining an octagonal stone set in the center of the gazebo, are unconcerned with human opinion.

Grass has grown over a memorial granite stone, and birds sing loudly this afternoon in a wood surrounding a quiet, sun-dappled clearing that features an ornate eight-sided gazebo which is lighted at night, sometimes.

Is this a story of action?

Of necessity? Activity?

Can we reanimate motionlessness?

We do fight—we do *that* much—mainly to kill each other over being right and over what we want.

To this writer's opinion, a cemetery is one of the calmest places we have in our constructed world. We've worked so hard to become so still.

This day, this time, the writer walks to the steps leading down and carefully avoids stepping on the different-sized milling black ants to squat and read the date on a memorial stone set at the entrance: *Sept. 30, 1979.*

A small red maple tree and nicely-selected accent plants adorn the gazebo like a halo. There is mulch there.

A couple had paid to build this gazebo; they were at least the major contributors. Their names are on the memorial stone. Or, the surviving spouse had paid for this visible testament to a formerly intact, purposeful and vibrant union of their lives in this passing act of what we call life. The writer wonders who yet lives in their family's tree.

Three millstones are tastefully placed among a shaded stand of evergreens by the side of the library near an asphalt parking area. The writer stands and leaves the memorial stone and gazebo behind, walking two hundred feet sedately, notebook in hand, head mostly down. He crosses a flat lawn and continues up a small hill to sit on the second millstone.

This millstone-turned-picnic-table rests directly beneath a large pine tree.

"I sit on the second millstone," the writer writes, looking around at the agreeable surroundings. He is alone, and finds this most agreeable.

Two blue postal mail boxes, transformed into book-drops, stand at attention and flank the sidewalk to the library's front doors. The writer checks his cheap prepaid cell phone: 2:32.

Almost time. The sale starts at three.

Breezes in the moving pine needles overhead and among the gently-waving deciduous leaves of the woods around these library grounds. Bird sounds. Stillness. Distant traffic noises.

Insects fly at the writer's head. He removes his baseball hat and waves it to discourage the possible biting flies, horseflies or mosquitoes. The library's condensing unit kicks on, blowing hot air onto the tender reaching shoots of a sapling growing close to the building.

Two black birds are soaring just over tree level. The writer had noticed their silent moving shadows earlier, and searched the sky. He caught glimpses of them moving through openings between branches. Not one cloud. It's mid-seventies in the shade and mid-80s in the sun. Fahrenheit. That's this writer's guess. It feels somewhat humid.

A thought occurs to go to his car to put away the spiral notebook he's writing in and to grab the empty cloth bags that he brought for the book sale. He is here, more than a hundred miles from his home, to buy other people's unwanted books.

Five minutes to go, he writes with his black ballpoint pen.

A fly had been pestering him at the second millstone table. He had sworn after swatting with his hat the third time. The writer moves to the millstone table nearest his car.

"God damn it," he addressed the fly. "I don't smell *that* bad."

A few more flies join their companion in landing on, and flying around, his head. Angrily, half-standing, the writer looks around in irritation and sees, four feet behind him, a black fly-coated writhing bundle at the base of the fir tree by the table.

No wonder, he thinks with disgust. He backs up, imagining where and what the flies had been crawling over and through before landing on his neck and ears.

A dead crow, completely covered with crawling flies.

"I bet *that* smells good enough for you, though," the writer says to the situation, to the flies, to the crows and to himself.

He walks away, finishing writing this sentence.

We're all in this together, he thinks, swatting a flying beetle dead that just landed on the right side of his chest.

The writer stops at his car, standing in the half-shade by his driver's side door. He flaps the spiral notebook closed and whispers, "Let's get out of here."

In ten minutes, he is leaning against a bookshelf and trying to read a book that he's removed from the shelf. A giant bespectacled woman in the waiting line tells the woman next to her, "This is where I dump my books."

"It's where I unload my inventory I don't move," she explains, boasting to all of those within earshot that her husband has dropped off more than 100 books during their last "dump."

Great, the writer thinks. Coming to a sale full of already picked-over books isn't going to be so good.

He'd seen the woman loading boxes and bags into a van from the side door of the library half an hour earlier while sitting on the first millstone table.

"Queen Picker" he christened this large, self-important-acting female. The sale opened, and now she was chirping important sounds at the library sale volunteers while fingering without interest through books. It's a farce. *No,* the writer corrected, *she's probably still looking to see what she missed.* He, along with most of the other book sale attendees, silently looks through the books, not finding much of interest.

After twenty-five paltry minutes, the writer checks out, paying for a disappointingly small bagful of books. A Charlie Brown cloud of disappointment hangs over his head as he returns to his car. He slides open the side door and places the books in a Postal Service plastic tub behind the driver's seat.

His baseball hat is on the passenger seat beside him. The writer backs the car over pine needles, and then drives off, GPS now set for "Home." The windows are open; his sunglasses are on. *Whadda you gonna do?* he thinks.

The disappointment cloud dissipates as he turns left and accelerates onto the road leading to the highway. In a few minutes he turns on the radio. On the way home he manages to stop at a few thrift stores and ongoing library sales where he finds a handful of more books.

Chapter 7 — Please Tell Me a Story

[vingt-neuf mai deux mille douze]

Why?

Because I want to be <u>entertained</u>.

What does <u>that</u> mean?

I want an <u>adventure</u>. And that means I want to encounter something new and unexpected. I want a vacation from having to face myself and what I'm used to. I want something *else*.

Why? What's the point in that?

I can't say, exactly. I don't like to think about it too much. I don't know—show me something <u>exciting</u>!

So, escaping boredom? Is that it? What is boredom, really? Feelings of revulsion? "Quiet desperation"? Are these feelings really feelings? Are they real?

Yes, yes, yes, yes, yes. I know how boredom feels; this doesn't mean that I understand it or anything else. In fact…. In fact, I don't <u>know</u> anything. I couldn't tell you the first thing about anything. I don't know anything for sure. Who *does*? Does anyone? I don't think anyone knows what anything means.

Who knows what's what, and why everything is the way it is? Do you think someone does?

In the history of every human that ever was, do people think or <u>know</u> that they know the score? How many of them actually do know? One? Not one?

If God told some of them what's going on, as they claim, how can they know it gave them good information? A god could be lying or wrong. Or, are gods incapable of lying or of being wrong? In any case, how could <u>you</u> know? You couldn't check the facts from a god because <u>your</u> information would always be second hand; you don't know first cause for yourself.

In the end you will believe whatever you do without knowing. Right? Even if you were God, or merely all-knowing, would you know for sure, somehow, or would you just believe that you're one hundred percent right? What is "right"?

Do all-knowing beings have flawless truth-telling senses, like we deluded believers do? Would God grow deaf to thinking after millions or billions of years? Is a billion years merely a year for a god? Or a minute? Has God fallen asleep and forgotten everything? Can you sleep if there's no time? Has God ever been awake? What would "awake" be to a god? Maybe <u>that's</u> what's going on. Maybe God has fallen asleep to escape boredom. If <u>you</u> were an all-powerful God who was wrong about something, who could tell you?

Oh, come on—just please tell me a story! Okay?

Okay.
Once upon a time….
There was once….
Once….

So, this story has a beginning?

….Yes.

And at the other end, an end?

Yes.

And something in between?

Yes.

And this whole universe is a story, isn't it? We're all characters. We're all part of a story, right now!

Yes.

And, in the beginning—at least we believe in a beginning—things "age" after all, don't they? In the beginning, there was such a thing as time. Once upon a time, time began. Time means progression, so there <u>must</u> *be a story now.*

What is progression? Can it exist all by itself? Is your God outside of time?

God is superior to time.

What if your God was time? What *is* time? Causality? Isn't that what we think God is? The cause of everything? What if we are living *inside* of God right now, like bacteria lives inside our intestines? We are living inside of time (we believe), don't we? Isn't that the inside of God? Are we not symbiotes within God? Does he need us as much as we need our bacteria, or as much as we need time?

What about the unbelievable cold void of space? Is *that* inside of God? How can we both—God and us—be inside of space? Aren't we supposed to be separated? Does space exist for God? Can God feel? What is a vacuum? Is it nothingness? Really? Does God contain nothingness?

The extreme opposite of an absence (a vacuum), is a black hole singularity that squeezes us into an impossible union with everything else.

Anyhow, you got me going there for a while; I still want a story—and I don't want to think anymore about all of this. Tell me a good story. Make it good. And don't forget: this is **God**. I demand obedience.

Alright.

Once upon a time there was a man—young in his mind and body—who said, "Tell me a story."

This man was unfamiliar with tragedies and with the resulting moods that accompany events in the lives of those who are a generation older than his self. Although young and inexperienced, he was deeply moody. He was a kaleidoscope of discontent, a cuttlefish of ever-shifting psychedelic psychological colorations lighting the blackness with a glow of constantly-altering hues, stunning wave fronts and subtle, then stark, ever-changing colors.

He had not lived long enough for his soil to grow into that sickly persistent flower—angst—moodiness, though, yes, yes; he had moodiness.

Sunset on his birthday meant something. The importance he infused into small rocks, fossils and other things he collected in a box echoed without end inside of his mind. A persistent afterimage remained whenever he closed his eyes. He carried all the images of everything he ever felt.

He lived through strongly-felt moods. Was his soul tainted, yet? Was he flooded by jaded acceptance of an unforgivable injustice? No. Contemplated negativity was irrelevant and bore no resemblance to his inner landscape. Everything wavered in the roiling heat of his moods.

He floated upside-down in a fishbowl of himself.

This is a story of youthful wordless passion and gravity.

There is no changing this boy-man, dreaming his tail-chasing profound reactions. What could possibly happen in this place of his own creation?

As winter snow cannot convince the grass to grow; and as the grass under a summer sun cannot yearn itself into brown lifelessness.

In the end, he melted. His green grew less green; a season approached that he could not have imagined. He grew soggy and formless. It was only then, that he could see things beginning to grow within, and on, his life.

Things like moss.

Chapter 8 — On the Eve of 45

[vingt-deux mai deux mille douze]

While you read this, I will be at least another year older. Two, in fact. You, too. Time marches on without, or even with, our cooperation.

"On the Eve of 45"

Waiting alone in the meeting room, the second hand on the cheap battery-powered wall clock on the right side of the door ticked loudly its metronome cadence.

"Fitting," he said to the room, to life and to the universe.

According to the date, and underlined by the regular ticking-by of days and years during this life, tomorrow he will be 45. This is the eve of that accomplishment.

"What does it matter?" he asks, waiting for the usual meditation on time, mortality and senselessness:

Where was I twenty years ago?

He thinks about that.

How bad will I feel in twenty years?

He thinks about that, too, and doesn't want to.

How good is it possible to feel?

He doesn't have much hope on that front.

What is life? Really...?

He thinks he knows. Finally.

In earlier versions, he gets up and *does* something. He explores the darkened auditorium beyond the meeting room door, walks the silent L-shaped hall holding his notebook and pauses to scribble words as the impulses appear on the surface of his pond-like mind.

"And now? On the eve of 45?"

His words settle on the oval, polished oak table before him, lying like a handful of wooden coins thrown there.

Two hours ago, while sitting in a swivel office chair in front of his computer monitor, he was typing barcode numbers from books to add to his online book seller account. A spray bottle of *Goo Gone* stood next to the kitchen scale on top of a ¼" thick sheet of Masonite screwed to the top of a ¾" sheet of plywood with rounded edges. This was his work desk, where he wrote, paid bills, corresponded and did books.

To the left of the computer screen, the plastic red scale weighs each bubble shipper-packaged book that he sends to South Dakota, California, Australia and Norway. He sells books all over the world. This afternoon, he finished entering the last of the new books that he'd bought at four recent book sales.

That moment he'll forget, he's pretty sure, and then he'll remember it some other time.

Once the last book was added to his virtual bookstore, a rushed early afternoon shower, tooth brushing (working from home affords such late rituals); and a 25-mile drive to the Paradox Book Store in Wheeling to leave a box of low-value books culled from his inventory. At a the Centre Market deli, he purchased small bags of Doritos and cheese popcorn, after which, he drove over to pay a visit to the book sale rack on the main floor of the Wheeling library. He bought a single 50-cent paperback, *The Soul of a New Machine* by Tracy Kidder.

As he headed over to the circulation desk to pay, he saw his future self packaging this book at his desk, weighing it and printing off a mailing label to tape onto the bubble shipper, noting a destination city, state or country and maybe reading the buyer's name before forgetting it immediately.

Utah. Swanson of Utah. Something like that, he thought.

What is *forgetting? What a miracle* remembering *is….*

Can I forget something I never consciously noticed?

At the meeting table, sitting with a pen poised over a spiral notebook, he didn't have answers to any of his questions. It felt important to ask, though. Accompanying the ticking of the wall clock was a silence that seemed to be slowly blanketing the sounds beneath a muted surface.

"Pond," he wrote. Somehow, he knew he would remember why he wrote it.

Tag words were good reminders, he knew. That's why multiple choice tests are so popular with teachers who don't want their students to abysmally fail their courses.

In the carpeted basement meeting room of the Wheeling library, *The Soul of a New Machine* on the surface in front of him, on his Eve of Imminent Olderness, he leans back in the reclining fabric-covered swivel chair. Library employees call this place "The Board Room."

The Meeting of the Minds Philosophic Inquiry Forum (M&M Philosophy) has met every Tuesday in this lower level for eight years. Running his weekly meetings—they run themselves, actually—he rides along, seated at a steering wheel that isn't connected to anything. It all seems like a dream.

In his spiral notebook, the almost-45-year-old takes a moment to write, "Got into a discussion with Don about his Follansbee, West Virginia Wheeling Pittsburgh Steel Corporation coke plant."

An hour after the meeting starts he writes,

"Tim showed us *Sacred Mirrors: The Visionary Art of Alex Grey* and told us about his own altered states of consciousness experiences in his mid-40s while working at Weirton Steel. Yodeling Dick came in and sat quietly, listened, and then told us about mental processes and insomnia."

That was all he wrote.

Chapter 9 — Gasoline Planet

[juillet deux mille douze]

Titan, the largest of Saturn's 62 moons, has a nitrogen atmosphere containing methane. The methane is converted into benzene, acetylene and propane. If the place had free oxygen and some lightening or static charge, you'd have a COLOSSAL Tiki torch. An atmosphere like Titan's *rains* these highly-refined fuels.

What if we lived on a flammable planet?

What if *our* world were made from gasoline? Like sculptures carved from fuel—even the houses would be made of solid gasoline.

If we carved these houses and machines and tools and books from solidified gasoline, what if we, the carvers, were also made from high-octane fuel? What if the clay we were formed from was really gummy gasoline?

All of this *is* true, but the question in *my* mind is: why do things burn? What does "burn" mean? What is going on? What *is* fire? In and of itself? Is it a "change of phase"? What does a change of phase *mean*? It looks to me like something is disintegrating.

Do we have photosynthesizing plants to thank for our version of fire? Without their output—oxygen— would we even *have* fire? Why does wrapping paper, newspaper, flour or sugar—or gasoline— "burn" so willingly? Surface area, accelerant, oxidizer, vaporization.... Okay, okay. Do human scientists *know* what is happening when a bomb ignites or a cozy fire crackles in our fireplace? They say they do. They sound like they do. I don't think they do.

Does a fire burn in space?

The sun burns, doesn't it? Oh. A nuclear reaction (sun) and a chemical reaction (campfire) are different things. Okay. Rockets burn, don't they? What about that candle I see flickering over there on the table? Chemical reactions... *right*....

In his equation, Einstein wrote that energy is equal to mass times the speed of light squared. $E=MC^2$. Really? *Really?* It must be; he said it, after all. My mind vaguely recalls the notion that mass can be converted into energy and energy into mass. Who does this "converting"?

I recall that it's a staggering amount of energy from each tiny bit of material—each cluster of atoms—that would be released if this material was ever "converted" completely into energy. A cube of sugar. A cup of gas. The energy that these things would put off....

What about the "energy" a sun puts off?

In the fireplace, burning logs, with the help of energy, or "fire," are converted into carbon dioxide, water and ash. Nothing is lost, even though "energy" radiates like a small sun from the fire. We're told that everything balances; this is what we discovered. Each grain of sand on a beach combines with others to make up a *lot* of mass. Everything combines with everything.

Scientists have come up with theories and principles based on meticulous observations. Their theories evolve to explain observed phenomena. They perform experiments on a smaller scale that validate predicted outcomes. They predict phenomena. They project their results onto a macro scale of solar systems, galaxies and the universe (or universes) and observe these things. My simple questions are an attempt to understand something fundamental beneath the "facts" of human-explained phenomena. Scientific facts are words. I know they mean something, but I wanted to *know*, firsthand, for myself, meaning itself.

"Einstein was the first scientist to propose his formula and the first to interpret mass–energy equivalence as a fundamental principle that follows from relativistic symmetries of space and time."

I can't *see* this. I like the sound of it, but I don't have the time spent in this speculative material to see or to feel any of this intuitively. What is going on when a flammable clay creature such as me, or an astrophysicist, intuitively *knows* what is happening in the center of a sun?

Our sun is a continuous "nuclear" explosion, we're told—this is an unbelievable release of energy. A continuous nuclear <u>fusion</u> explosion. Fusion is when two atomic nuclei press or squeeze into each other to produce a new, singular, kind of heavier atom. Energy, resulting, is released.

This fusing of two nuclei happens at tremendous speeds when not in the extreme high pressure environment of a gravitationally massive sun; it happens fast there, too; this fusing always happens because of a "fast" smashing of atomic elements; but, in the case of our hydrogen bombs, these elements are slammed together at relativistic speeds (a significant percentage of the speed of light), such speeds made possible by the detonation of a high energy, conventional, shaped explosive forcing its energy inward, mimicking, for the briefest of nanoseconds, the unthinkable pressures existing within and on a fusion-burning star. This triggering explosion ignites, by fusing two lighter atoms together, a chain-reaction sparker we label with the words: "nuclear bomb." A star is born.

A star, with its spacetime-warping gravity, is a colossal factory of heavier elements. Long-dead stars are responsible for *our* existence and *our* planet, which is comprised of the elements such as iron, nickel, calcium and carbon. These "heavy" elements are formed in the hearts of stars, which then were blasted outward at the ends of the stars' lives.

Our sun is a main-sequence star, and thus generates its energy by the nuclear fusion of hydrogen nuclei into helium. In its core, the Sun fuses 620 million metric tons of hydrogen each second.

Does the "fire" of a star produce mass as a by-product? *Uh… yes. I just said that.*

Living plants don't grow in our sun, do they? Sunfire obviously "burns" in space without the oxygen made by plants. Nuclear fusion exists without oxygen.

Heavier atoms, those groups of atoms called "elements," were only, so we're told, manufactured in the extreme pressure and heat existing in the cores of stars which then blew themselves apart in supernovae explosions, spraying their interior contents outward, away, into the vast airless cosmos at the moment of their deaths.

On the Cornell Center for Materials Research "Ask a Scientist" internet webpage, a scientist writes that "fire" as we know it doesn't exist. In fact, all burning is quite simple. "In combustion, old bonds are broken and new bonds are made, but the atoms remain the same."

I know, I know—chemical reactions are not the same as nuclear reactions. I just don't buy it. I think we're missing what's going on. Could we understand just any *one* thing? *Really* understand?

Nothing changes at a fundamental level. The universe is a giant aquarium. It's not possible for something different, or outside of it, to happen. Is this right?

How *could* something totally different happen in a closed system? Nothing, really, *goes* anywhere. Everything's always here in the aquarium, only moved around. The scales are permanently balanced.

Back to stars. Their non-oxygen burning inferno leads to the "creation" of matter such as ourselves. *What is creation? What is matter? What does it matter?* Is everything just another, bigger, aquarium?

Apparently, "creation" is another manifestation of same-old, same-old. Snow or ice, water or vapor— they're all "different" but the same— what we refer to as water. And *matter....* Well, I'll leave matter alone for a while.

Heavier material (matter) created in stars is reorganized to form our planet in the shape of trees, mushrooms, magazines and rainbows—which can, in turn, be burned and dissolved into blazing energy that becomes seeming nothingness. Fusion and Fission. Coming together and blowing apart. Energy. What *is* energy?

From my point of view all of this is strange. What *is* strange? What does "strange" mean, in and of itself? Information and concepts that don't jibe with my "understanding" of specific observable phenomena. *Understanding*? What about *that* notion that we take for granted without examining?

Where *did* the chunk of firewood go? I see ashes and the soaring embers. I'm left with an impression that I've been a witness to something more significant than I can comprehend.

"Comprehend"? Can a star comprehend itself intuitively while it burns?

I am a small collection of ingredients from the life cycle of stars. A tiny portion of their family tree. An ember. A tiny, tiny particle within their generations. Heavier elements organized into the shape and structure of my body and nervous system.

I write these words longhand on the pages of a cheap spiral notebook—highly flammable material, of course. Look up at the nearby sun. What could you throw into *that* furnace which *wouldn't* catch fire? This ballpoint pen? My clothes and a frumpy-looking cloth-covered reclining swivel chair?

Galaxies are colliding in slow motion as they revolve silently around their own centers; they are consumed, ultimately, by the super massive black holes at their nexus—and these black holes merge. Mass converts to energy, transforms into singularities of nothingness so completely homogenously squeezed into oblivion that no such thing is able to exist—including "there." That's what black holes seem to be.

When our star reaches the end of its life and goes nova, exploding and blowing outward from its center, vaporizing and burning away its inner and outer planets (its children), then everything we are will be reduced to dust and blown outward like dandelion seeds. We will become a ghost nebula among a cosmos of other nebulae smeared across the backdrop of forever, swirling, then sinking into another gravity well of proximity, be it black hole or newly-formed star. We'll be the marker dye in a vortex of blazing creation and immolation.

How can I, this flammable, individualized, conglomerate, *think* any of this? Is *thinking* itself burning? Where does this energy, this burning, this thinking *go*?

I am an ember soaring above a campfire, pondering its existence in relation to a guessed-at, speculated-about universe before growing dimmer and fading into darkness (for a while, before my next material incarnation).

We *are* all one, non-dualist Advaitists tell us.

We *choose* many things—like writing about life and about fire—and we're going to burn with all of our books. This book-burning universe defies definition. Turning pages into dust slowly or rapidly; it's all a change of phase.

We are tiny sparks, small suns that don't explode all at once, but instead "burn" slowly. Our aging process is a burning. We'll all be, one day, in the center of a star, or, obliterated endlessly as we pass through the event horizon of a space-less, timeless, black hole.

What, *exactly*, is time? Can it exist? Or burn?

We "used to be" something very different from what we are. Do we remember? Not just back in Roman times or during the Stone Age. You and I have resided for countless millennia in the center of once-living stars, once, long, long ago. We were all present at the beginning, in that grand birth spasm of our current observable universe (even though most of what we're "observing" in the heavens, right now, is already millions, even billions, of years old and gone already).

Where were we before the beginning? *What* were we? How many fingers did we have? In one of our numerous incarnations of a universe gone by, did we ever wonder these sorts of things? Do we keep forgetting that we used to wonder?

Languishing in the primordial all-is-the-same soup inside of the last, first, and last again black hole of the universe before its first beginning? Before it collapsed another last time in a rush to consume itself? *What happens next?* We growing-colder embers <u>always</u> ask those "before" and "next" questions. We always ask. We cannot conceive of a snake eating its own tail, where nothing begins or ends. Can we?

Steven Hawking, in his *A Brief History of Time*, says there doesn't *have* to be a beginning of time, or even a beginning of anything. On the surface of an inflated red balloon—or on a globe or within our expanding universe—there *is* no "beginning," he says. No start point on a ball. I think that's what he says.

"Beginning" is not a valid concept in such an all-is-one dimension. We yearn for a beginning, though, a first cause. Why? What we *really* want is something more complete than any beginning or end is capable of being for us.

Time and all beginnings and endings are arrayed on a single unbroken surface. Time is a phenomenon seen dimly, through ourselves.

We see a spinning wheel in brief flashes of stillness as our eyes track, desperately, for purchase.

Who *made* this shrinking and growing balloon we're all living on, or living inside of? Who made us? Are we always asking the wrong questions because they're all we can ask? Does what we're looking for automatically exist, *because* we are able to ask about it?

If primordial dust results from burning things, from things phase-changing, and all these things come from a rebounding, exploding, inside-out, invisible, unreal black hole universe, then where did everything come from? Can't we *please* ask?

No.

Stop.

Asking.

Questions.

Some (who couldn't know) say that God is immune to, and outside of, time. They state that God is the creator, and that we are all merely parts of God. I that say maybe we're all God's... output. Maybe God is a giant earthworm, or an immortal goose, and we have all been "processed."

God's belly expands and contracts, expands and contracts.

Does *someone* have the BIG picture? Does the Earthworm know something for sure?

I ate my lunch and soon I will hike up a hill. I'm an internal combustion machine; my cells "burn" glucose to propel this pen, to think, to breathe and to hike up hills.

Nothing has a steady state. *Everything* burns all of the time. Radioactivity—the invisible decay of unstable elements—is a "burning." Does God rot? Can God decay? Can God burn? Is God a giant universe candle? Where does God or the wax go when the universe disappears? If God's belly *is* the universe, does God get indigestion?

I—a small part of a universe—*feel* a permanence. This feeling has been in me for some

years and I *know* it but I can't explain it. Some part—
a steady-state condition inside of me—is apparently
ininflammable. Unburnable.

Impossible.

Yes.

And yet.

Burning from the inside out, I nevertheless *am*.
Gasoline is not my fuel. Gasoline *is* me. I burn.

Nothing remains of me.

Nothing, including Unknowing, "burns" away.

Everything is gone, except for *Yes*

No.

Yes.

Chapter 10 — "Light, an autobiography"

[dix-sept août mai deux mille douze]

Riding on an unbroken beam of me, I ricochet from the airless, brilliantly-cratered face opposite a fairer planet.

In a matter of seconds (1.3 seconds to be precise) I shoot into the open end of a ten-inch reflecting telescope, smoothly bouncing from the parabolic primary and flat secondary mirrors facing each other. I am squeezed tightly into focus and then slip through the right eye of a momentarily-distracted yet interested child standing on tiptoes, peering into—*what?...* with their mouth open at the utter blackness of mystery surrounding the gigantic hovering moon.

Inside, I find myself in a medium of electrical biological liquids, flowing molecules passing through ganglia, where parts of me are pulled away to be stored and absorbed and memorized inside of quivering cells, each, a cosmic island.

My essential core continues unabated. I funnel laser-like into the pineal region of the growing eight year old brain where ALL is brightness. Various parts of me are deflected, swirling and sliding along the curved, gelatinous walls of inner formlessness. Bored easily, seeking openness, I merge into a return line and exit a second parallel ocular portal.

I shoot out from under a slowly-closing eyelid and angle off a puddle of liquid on the sidewalk in front of *Smart Centre Market "Wheeling's Interactive Science Store,"* across from where the owner and his brother-in-law have black tube reflecting telescopes set up forty feet apart. The owner's device is aimed at the moon—that's where I came from—and his wife's brother sits on a folding chair next to the five-foot-long telescope pointing at Saturn. Passers-by are encouraged to look through side-mounted eyepieces.

Faster than anything else, I pass through a transparently frozen plate of vibration-sensitive silicon dioxide sodium oxide. Warping slightly, I find a polished slice of quartz and bounce away, away, away.

Glancing through a second plate of warping clearness, I feel its tug on the way out. I also feel tired. I always feel tired.

I have never stopped. I am unable to slow and I feel the pull of everything. Everything I have passed through since the beginninglessness of myself. I am trapped in my speeding freedom.

Faster, by far, than everything else put together, I am singular and alone.

Singular. Diffracted parts of me are sprayed everywhere. I feel everything. I am separate and uncatchable. Connected, bound and enslaved by my nature.

I long for an end.

My journey is not going to end.

Reflecting from the edge of a mirrored surface on the side of a ground-effect petrochemical combusting conveyance fabrication, I aim higher, rebounding from a tall structure to another moving winged conveyance fabrication that travels through the thinner atmosphere multiple units above the planet's surface. I shoot into an oval transparent opening and flash the length of a narrow machine carrying two hundred sitting beings. Restless, I pass *away*, through another opening.

Far....

Beyond the planet, in the blink of an eye, in the open stillness of unseen relative energies, I bask in the silence of all things and fall back into memory-less no-thing being as I race on, like always, at top speed.

Chapter 11 — "Paris, My Paris"

[dimanche, dix-sept septembre deux mille douze]

Everything is real.

Green leaves, oak trees, blue azure sky, the sun's white highlights on the right side of everything. A car slowly rolls past, twenty feet behind my head, crunching gravel accompanies a low dust cloud pulled along in its wake before dispersing and settling.

Large fifth wheel campers with accordion sides popped out, rest in a row under the morning sun in front of the shade line from a tall row of massive Sycamores along the river.

I smell, faintly, the natural gas tag odor from the *Columbia Gas Adaline Compressor Station*, three or four hundred yards away upstream, on the other side of the river.

A slight breeze. The river is low.

We're near Cameron, West Virginia, in a very hilly, wooded, rural area. An aging wrought iron bridge spans this creek-like river. Loose boards, laid on edge, rattle, shake and clank when cars or off-road four-wheelers roll across. A single-engine prop plane drones a few thousand feet overhead.

This day is perfect and timeless.

It reminds me of Ernest Hemingway's memoir of his observations and experiences in 1920s Paris. I read *A Movable Feast* before I went to Paris and again, sometime after. Neither time was intentional.

I have been to Paris during three decades in my lifetime—in my 19th year, my 32nd year and in my 43rd year—probably five separate times, altogether. At least.

Even before I went to Paris myself, I was nostalgic for Hemingway's fall-time Paris of the 20s when I read his *Feast*. He writes that way. Nostalgia. I experienced his nostalgia through the times he was writing about. I'm a sucker for nostalgia; it doesn't take much. Smells do it. Fall is my favorite time of year, followed closely by winter. Spring and summer are nice, too.

Now I have my own nostalgia for Paris, and my own places, in that city, that I prefer to visit and spend time in. There are always new places to find, and new experiences to have in all the new and old places. My own memories are there of things done and felt under bridges arching over le Seine, in cafés, atop monuments and underground.

I have been in Paris during the damply cold, rainy fall; in the frigid, dry, windy snow of winter, in early spring and in the humid, sultry hot baking summer. I carry my Paris with me. I barely know it, but *my* Paris is always there and always here.

My older son, Guillaume, is watching a downloaded Steelers football game on his I-Pad on the row of seats in front of me. His younger brother, Ben, is playing "Parking Mania" on the I-Pod he bought from his brother with his own allowance money after Gui upgraded to a reconditioned I-Pad with *his* self-earned money.

I am lying in the back of our Pontiac minivan with the rear hatch lifted. On my back, with a folded boy's Pittsburgh Steelers jacket under my head, my head sticks out of the back of the van and I'm writing on a cheap spiral notebook held up over my head at arm's length.

A group of 14 ladies is gathered under the picnic shelter with my artist wife, Andrée, eighty feet away in this *Fish Creek Country Store & Campgrounds* rural park area. Nervous cackles and laughter fade into silence as Andrée's voice intones her painting instructions to a group of women wearing aprons sitting or standing in front of canvases.

I have just placed a glow-in-the-dark Nerf football under my head so that I can write easier. Gui is sniffing a lot as he watches his game. I tell him to blow his nose.

We live fifty miles away, on the other side of a much bigger river than the creek flowing behind the row of campers; we live on the other side of the wide, quick-flowing Ohio. We live in Ohio, in our own ridgeline village of Flushing. There aren't as many trees where we live as there are here because much of the land near our home has been strip mined. At our home, as I lay in the car here, writing, and as Andrée runs a painting party, Mike, our English Labrador, is waiting in our house with two cats who are sisters. I know that after cars pause at the uphill Black Oak Drive intersection within sight of our house, Mike looks up, listening, when engines rev and vehicles pull onto our street and motor past.

If we had to walk home, it would probably take us two or three days. It's a long, winding way through these hills, down into the river valley and back up through more hills to the top of ridges again.

I pause from writing this to respond to Gui's questions about wanting to watch the Pittsburgh Steelers game in an hour. I say that we can listen to the beginning of the game on the van radio because it's unlikely we'll be home soon. It would take us an hour of steady driving simply to get home, I explain. I can tell that the social painting party is only halfway finished. I reassure Gui that we'll be able to watch a good part of the game at home. He is disappointed and unconsoled.

My arms are tired now from holding up this spiral notebook. I wish that I could put it down and relax into the moment, on this day, in this life, in this place.

So I do.

Chapter 12 — "Crows Talking"

[dimanche, vingt-quatre septembre deux mille douze]

Start.

Mt. Olivet.

Crows *caw*—... *caw*—... *caw*—... up in the trees. Some leaves are turning orange. These are oak trees, I think. There is some automobile traffic on the roads down below, and along here, to my left.

I have pulled onto the side of the road. The edge of the asphalt paving is thick and broken from cars doing this at the top of the hill above the baseball field. The grass here is worn away in a line from the right wheels of cars. Dusk is an hour or so away.

Asphalt, power poles, auto sounds. Sounds of tires, motors and muffled radios. Wind blowing an American flag in front of the Mt. Olivet United Methodist Church on the other side of Route 88, a two-lane winding rural highway down *there*, just past the ball field in the flat.

Now the flag hangs still. Now it's moving.

I'm wearing shorts. I feel a coolness on my legs as a breeze comes in through the open car windows. I smell burning wood. *Nice.* I always like that.

A lawn mower drones to itself in the distance. I turn my head very slowly, triangulating with my ears to pinpoint the direction. *Okay. Over there.*

Dramatic-looking clouds overhead. *No one will know what I mean by this.* Some sprinkles of rain spot the windshield.

What isn't *perfect?*

In the shifting light and in the tree branches again, in the leaves; what *isn't* supposed to be? Even the flag, the ball field and the broken asphalt.

Earlier, close to the edge of the Ohio River in Moundsville, West Virginia, ten miles south along the river from Wheeling and maybe six miles east from this small park in Mount Olivet, I sat in the waning noon-day sun on a seat swing in the cool river breeze across from a bend in the river near the 12th Street Bridge. It's a park area there, under that bridge, with a handful of evenly-spaced swinging seats for two people in a row, each facing the river. On the opposite side of the river, a few hundred yards away, stands a closed-down coal-fired power plant with train tracks, buildings and a large smoke stack. *Everything* is on the other side of something else.

Motorboats, aiming upriver, north, toward Wheeling, chop against the current and skip over the marching southbound ripples. Kids have played at the riverside park playground recently. A family reunion is winding down at a shelter on the edge of two parallel rows of tall trees that lead to the riverside yacht club and restaurant. There was a fishing derby still going on, and at the concrete boat ramp, a man with a clipboard sitting in a folding chair eyed me suspiciously (I was standing nearby, writing in this spiral notebook).

That was then. *Here,* now, the flag on its pole in front of the church down there waves majestically. Does this mean that patriots are attending services? Down there, I see cars parked in the side church parking lot.

The fence-enclosed diamond and field in the flat grass-covered area below are empty. I think about running the bases there. Another time, I probably would. Most times when I drive by, there is practice or a game. A perfectly-formed oak tree stands sentinel, mid-way up this hillside, between two towering metal sports field light poles and me.

I smell the smoke again. Incinerating sticks and boards, now, I'd guess. Cured, dried wood. Today is the first day of fall.

Were I to fly, unharassed by the crows in the trees and by those circling high up there, I could look down and see the top of this car and the small Mt. Olivet Park with its picnic shelter on the hill under the trees across from me overlooking the ball field from another vantage point along this higher ground. I'd look down from soaring effortlessly and see other cars moving past my parked car, their brake lights on, as they slow down to the "T" intersection and turn left or right on 88. A few cars might even pull into the church parking lot—or leave it. Some would make their way up this steep road.

I'm sure I'd feel the air—much colder several hundred feet up—as a pressure on my face. My eyes would water because I would probably forget to put on my sunglasses before climbing high past the treetops. I'm not used to moving this fast through the air without sunglasses. Driving my car, when I stick my head out the window, I usually have sunglasses on. Flying above the circling crows, as fun as it is, I would probably spend too much time regretting not having those glasses. Tears would be streaming back from the outside edges of my eyes. After a while, I'd get over this disappointment and keep flying.

September 24th.

What?

NOW.

Wind rustles the oak leaves in the trees in front of me and alongside my car. The flag down there waves, rippling back and forth. Now it's still; each time, it's different. Mostly green, but yellow, orange and burgundy—these are the colors of the leaves in the trees within sight, and overall, in all the distances I can see.

What if I lose this notepad? It would be like a raindrop on my windshield. You would never know what I noticed while sitting here.

A woman climbs slowly up the concrete stairs with her hand on a rusted metal tube handrail. She opens a worn aluminum storm door of the house on the edge of the road, on the other side of the street and down hill from me. She's not old, but she labored up those steps—she *is* pretty fat—and she paused a lot. Now she's inside her level house on this inclined hill.

In another place I know, a young man paces all day long in front of his house. A young dark-haired man with a slow, deliberate arm-swinging, loose-elbowed relaxed pace. He *used* to walk all the way down our busy road, route 331, starting from his house, then up past the prison before the highway exit on I-70 westbound.

From his house in Donnerville (just a name by some houses that you drive by) to the exit on the highway, he walked back and forth all of the time; I'd seen him walking at different places along that stretch of road at different times. It's five miles each way, from the house where I think he lives to the prison. The coal trucks blow down that road all day long. That young man walked in the heat of summer the dead of winter. No shirt in the heat, and wearing just a knit hat and a hooded sweater in the cold. He must have been told that he can't walk there anymore because now we've got a lot of gas field machinery going down the roads constantly. He must feel like a caged stallion now. I haven't seen him on the road for a while.

Crazy?

Sometimes, like sitting here, I think I could—I should—just stay in one place and do nothing ever again. That's how it feels. *Sometimes I really feel that I should*. I really should. The smell coming from over there now, from that stovepipe sticking out of the side of the shed-like building across the road from me, tells me that the fire has gone out. It's that smell that comes from smoldering ends of logs in a campfire in a damp forest in the morning.

In a minute, I'll walk over to that picnic shelter. The terrain here is like a bowl, with the baseball field in its bottom and a picnic shelter and my car along the rim.

A lawnmower is making some noise beyond that house still.

Clouds, darkly, over there, and some blue sky and whiter clouds just overhead.

That flag is really wagging its tail. Now it's stopped. Now it's stretched out tight in the wind. Each time, different.

I see the black birds up there. The grass in this park is cut. Probably last week sometime.

Better walk now, while I can, before I get a call and drive off to go help Andrée take down the painting class easels and fold up taped-down drop cloths covering the deck behind that house where she's teaching people in the approaching dusk how to paint a picture of wine bottles.

Okay.

Chapter 13 — "Worth It"

[à peu pres septembre deux mille douze]

I have never wondered at my head making sense of everything—it just does. But now I wonder.

Just on the edge of the road, on the upper end of a sloping lawn, a young man stands, flying a remote-control helicopter, hovering it upside-down.

He pulls loops with the 20-inch-long helicopter as I roll slowly by and admire his precision flying. The miniature aircraft is performing maneuvers about 30 feet above a slanted lawn.

At the end of this narrow, nearly one-lane lane, I turned the car around on some gravel and a surprising (to me) dog barked when I drove past on my way out. He didn't make a sound on my way *into* the cul-de-sac, so I had dismissed him as a quiet dog; his sudden barking didn't go along with my pigeonholed assumption. A Siberian Husky with powdered blue eyes, a unibrow of black facial markings and a tightly curled tail.

> *Amazing underwater diving adventures? Cross-country solo hikes over breathtaking mountain passes? What is worth spending one's life energy doing? What isn't?....*

Surprising encounters with unexpected fill-in-the-blanks? Unexpected accidents? Heroic struggles? *Bien sûr.* Sure.

I could sit all day in this car on the side of a remote ridge road while waiting for Andrée to finish her painting party in the carpeted basement of a lady named Janet.

I had set up for Andrée—overlapping drop cloths secured with painter's masking tape; covering tables with plastic tablecloths; carefully-placing chairs, easels and canvasses; putting bottles of paint on each table; staging paintings along the walls to decorate; connecting Janet's iPhone to a speaker system for ambience music.

Each time is different and unique to the location; each place we set up for has its own circumstances—not enough room, hauling boxes up too many narrow steps, shifting furniture, setting up outdoors with the wind blowing canvasses over, poor lighting indoors and vainly searching for lamps. On and on. *Und so weiter.*

I need to work on my book when I get home [*A Handyman's Common Sense Guide to Spiritual Seeking*]. It's about action, I hope. It's a book about taking action in one's own life, possibly for the first time, and being one's own captain. Steering one's own boat. Making one's *own* way in this life, deciding things without always giving the decision keys of your destiny to another—to an advisor, an authority or to peer pressure. The book is almost done; one more pass through, I hope. I'm in the editing phase, which means reading through and trying to make it just right.

I'm sure I could work on the manuscript for two or three or four or five or six more passes. I'd probably destroy it completely. Like *this* one; I'd edit to oblivion. Or I could start over again, and start over again. And start over. But for now, it's probably better to do one last pass and put my editing pen down. *Have to stop* sometime. Like a painter never satisfied.

What do I want *Handyman* to reflect?

I want to erase everything that isn't True, leaving only the Most Important Thing.

What *is* worth saying? With the best of intentions, what could I possibly say to *you* that is worth your time listening to? What could I *say* that means something? In the best of moods, with the best of luck, maybe I can say something good. I could say this one thing and nothing—nothing—else.

A blue sky. White, puffy, eternally-changing clouds.

An airplane sound floating in and out as the winds blow, like an auditory smoke trail thinning through the sky. I go for a walk across a nearby field into a meadow. I stand for minutes on end, noticing bees in the flowers around my feet, and stare over at sunlit trees.

What *is* worth reading? *Ich weiß es nicht.*

Chapter 14 — You Will Leave

[mardi, treize novembre deux mille douze]

You came into this place through shocked trauma, pulled from the soothing warmth of impressions and vagueness into a dream of light.

In death, you will return to vagueness, through a portal of your passing.

Mouth remains open or mouth shut (likely open). Eyes still open or eyes shut (fifty-fifty on this).

You will leave this place the way you came.

No. You will dissolve. You will pass into oblivion.

In the end, entropy rules—especially in *your* case. You're the only one here; the rest of us are supporting actors, if that.

In another's birth now, and later, when you're gone, there is flight and movement and blazing energy. The end of *your* ember is a ceasing; a dying light.

How many ways has this been said or felt?

I remember sitting in a laundromat eighteen years ago as if it were this afternoon, as if I were sitting there, now. I don't remember the weather. Today is cold, and it grows darker every day. It is a Tuesday evening.

Drama.

Youth.

Health.

Virtue.

Ideals.

Beliefs.

Hope.

Addiction.

In the end, you will be freed from everything.

Your friends are your co-embers in this brief glowing life of **yours**. You rise and fall in one another's presence—soaring in heat and sinking in coolness, individually together.

Your parents wink out before you do, and your children rise and fall, with luck, after your light has grown dark. Of course, it happens in many different ways. Every different way is possible—but always the same.

Your friends will die by your side, or you will die by theirs, or you'll go first and they won't know, or they'll go first and you'll find out later.

"I'm addicted to life."

Who ever *says* that?

To occupy oneself with, or to involve oneself in, something habitually or compulsively. That's one definition of "addicted."

Habit: an action or activity I do repeatedly.

Compulsion is something I am... compelled to do. When I cease to be attached to or addicted to myself and my habit of having interests, then I cease to be "alive" in the same static, self-referencing way.

*

Will you hold this?:

A boy finds a bottle lying half-covered in the sand near some beachgrass. On the shore the surf washes its cadence and interacts with itself, rolling, washing, and grinding shells and flotsam in a repetitive, eternal motion.

The empty Pepsi bottle is picked up from the warm sand. Contentment flows through the young boy's soul. He squats and sets the bottle upright on the dampness just beyond the advancing and retreating water. A hand, holding sand, lets granules sift into the rounded top to cascade musically inside with a hollow *schuss*.

Sand fills the bottle, is poured out, forming a pile. Again and again.... The pile grows.

Later, small shells fill the bottom of the cylindrical plastic shape.

The boy holds a hand on top of the bottle and shakes it. This, and its resultant sound, goes on for some time.

The bottle is filled again, this time with broken shells, flattened pebbles, worn wood fragments and small pieces of sand-tumbled glass.

He pours them, shaking them into a pile next to the sand-only pile.

He goes over to the incoming waves with the empty bottle. He wades in, ankle deep, and holds the bottle under the surface just after a wave. A small amount of water and swirling sand is held up to glitter in the sun. It is a somewhat cloudy mixture.

The boy puts a hand on top of the bottle opening, holds the bottom with his other hand, and shakes the water repeatedly. He stops and peers into the upheld container. The sun glints from a water droplet on the bottom edge of the upheld bottle and causes its swirling, light-brown suspended contents to glow.

Water poured out again. Bottle refilled. Contents poured onto the top of the dry sand pile. Refilled. Poured again. Again and again and again. The sand pile is slumped, water-logged and spreading.

Empty bottle is impulsively tossed into the surf, and then retrieved by the running, cautiously-furtive boy. Thrown further—almost too far. Wading waist-high, then even deeper, with an incoming wave;

fearfully grabbing the bottle just before it moves away.

Back on the wet sand. Listening to the open end of the recently-emptied bottle. Fascination! This rapt listening goes on for a long time....

Blow, now, across the open top of the sand-encrusted plastic bottle. Most of the sand there blows away. Some of it sticks with the seawater. *Blow*. A sound is repeated again and again; higher with more water, deeper with less water; this is discovered.

Back on the dry beach; pour sand into the bottle with cupped hands. Wade again into the surf. Sand-brown water is added to the container by submerging it under incoming waves.

Walking contentedly ashore, shaking the bottle, watching the swirling sand and water, placing the bottle carefully on dry sand and laying alongside, head on one hand with elbow embedded in warm sand. Wet legs dry in the sun and wind. Lying on his side, watching the bottle.

Lying on his stomach, with clasped hands under chin, he watches the settled, submerged sand in the bottle and the clearing water. He waits.

The water clears. For a long, long time he watches the swirling particles, willing them to stop their movement.

It's a little ocean, he knows.

One after the other, other things happen, and the sun shines, and the wind blows steadily, and the surf crashes in and retreats in cadence. A long, timeless motion.

The sun, above all, the sun.

The constant, eternal sounds of the surf.

The wind blowing grains of sand; always blowing. Always.

The seagulls watching from above.

Now completely dry, lying on his back, the boy, with warmed arms stretched out at his sides, is looking up at the blue sky and a few starkly white clouds.

Following an impulse, he stands. Very slowly. With great effort.

Knees, shoulders, elbows and ankles ache with well-established osteoarthritis. The sun bakes his browned, wrinkled, spotted skin. He brushes sand away from his sagging chest and dry swim trunks. Spare wisps of hair on top of his head move with the offshore breezes. His head is warmed by the blazing star.

There is no bottle. No pile of sand or any pile of pebbles and shells now.

Floating specks move liquidly across the man's vision, matching his old eyes' movements as they track the blurred, bright-sky distance. He turns slowly in a circle, feet corkscrewing into the burning surface sand and deeper, into the beginning of coolness below. He squints against the sun and wind.

The endless horizon of the sea.

The hot sand and the wind and sun.

That's all.

*

Merci.

Chapter 15 — A Blade Hanging, Overhead

[trois décembre deux mille douze]

From the super-highway of his indestructible assumptive youth, one young man was detoured onto a pot-holed, dead-end side road.

Blindsided: Lifting a Life Above Illness: A Reluctant Memoir was written by producer and journalist Richard Cohen, a man with Multiple Sclerosis. In his book, he details his personal life-reaction to the progression of a debilitating affliction which intermittently undermines his physical stability and self-image by drastically affecting sight, balance and muscle control.

It isn't hard to imagine refusal, avoidance, neglect, indignation, despair, rage, depression, reluctance, impotence, indifference, indolence and acceptance of one's own personal, unavoidable, destiny when repeatedly confronted by the pounded-home, gradually-dawning knowledge of the one-way detour one has chanced onto, of steadily-reducing independence and increasingly-progressive loss of sight, body control and, above all, one's sacrosanct mental faculties.

The first time I heard Bart Marshall, a thoughtful acquaintance of mine, utter the phrase: "We're trapped in a dying animal," I really enjoyed this threatening-sounding metaphor. It sounded somewhat scary. An animal—any will do—wounded and lying and dying over a period of hours or days. We're all going to do that, of course; we're doing that now, but it sounds so foreign and so unexpected when phrased this way: "trapped in a dying animal."

Sting, bass player and front man for *The Police*, wrote his hit song, "Spirits in the Material World" for his band's 1981 album, *Ghost in the Machine*. We are spirits in a material world, he says. That sounds hopeful.

Even the "trapped in a dying animal" comment sounds sort of hopeful; as if we were somehow separate and capable of jumping overboard with the rats when the ship finally sinks below the surface. *As if*. We aren't even as removed as the slave chained to the oar. We're the oar itself and the self-same side stove-in ship, too.

Each of Cohen's reflexive coping responses—anger, denial, indifference—was a line of defense indiscriminately plowed over like an ant colony's labor-intensive excavations by an insensitive Fate? Call it fate, if it helps to feel better about the bad things that happen to us unexpectedly. Like the besieged town's defenses being effortlessly batted aside by an overwhelming enemy force.

Inevitable.

This is the scenario each of us will face sooner or later.

A guillotine, slowed one hundred thousand times, is a curiosity hanging overhead. I notice it; I am briefly intrigued, and then my thoughts re-turn to other things.

We walk, I think, with our personal slanted blades poised at varying distances above us. We've grown accustomed to this presence—if we've noticed it at all. The triangular shadow becomes a comforting familiarity. Mortality holds us down, keeping us grounded so we don't float away.

One day, I will face my doom... *my destiny*.... Fate.... But not today; not now.

I *am* facing it now, though, but it's moving so slowly and I have such a short attention span that I am unable to appreciate the importance of this approaching bus....

This guy started his young man's life with that MS blade hanging just a foot or so above his head—that's all—just a foot. Too close to see, maybe. Being young, he was carefree and immortal—but not for as long as he probably would have liked. A thin pressure against the back of his neck was met by mild indifference, impatience, irritation and actively ignoring it.

So slow as to seem motionless, this blade continued its downward pressure against his neck, right in the center back there.

What does it feel like for this to be carried to its destination? This relentless doom? It feels the same way for each one of us; we just don't pay attention until it's too late. And who in the world would *want* to pay attention in the middle of this game? "Pay attention." Who could? Pay attention. When does an intimation of mortality become an experienced reality? *Where* is that cross-over? Pay atten....

Would we—did Cohen—grow around this steadily-worsening affliction to a sense of invulnerability, this blade of mortality, like every tree grows around those nooses, those abandoned swing ropes? What will *we* do when the swing rope is forgotten and left knotted around our necks? The answer: what we *always* do.

We will do exactly as this MS guy, who is growing blinder each day, has done. We will face, bravely or un-bravely, into our oncoming oblivion. We will turn away until we no longer have an "away" to turn to. We all experience this utterly solitary activity, but we remain cocooned within our own reactions to this, our personal, shared plight.

*

On Mount Everest and K2—the two tallest mountains on Earth—mountain climbers enter a region above 26,000 feet called the "Death Zone," into which they venture on their way to the summit and back. Running quickly into space and back without a proper spacesuit is essentially what they are doing.

High altitude pulmonary edema (HAPE) and high altitude cerebral edema (HACE)—fluid accumulating in the lungs or in the brain—are looming threats that add their weight to that slowly-descending blade over each high climber.

Everyone who climbs knows this; each one is initiated into the fraternity of those-who-have-faced-the-nearness-of-one's-mortality. The lottery odds are favorable.

The human body dies rapidly in the Death Zone. More rapidly than normal. *Much* more rapidly. The guillotine's downward movement becomes perceptible. Some notice it, ignore it, and continue farther than it is truly possible for them to survive and the blade drops smoothly, slicing through their thread, leaving them a frozen testament in mid-stride on the uncaring, ice- and snow-covered mountain.

"Lucky" ones run up, suffer unimaginably, and hurry back down to sea level where their bodies repair and heal themselves as well as possible. Eventually, their guillotine blade slows again to an apparent standstill—although noticeably nearer to the tops of their heads.

The Death Zone.

Where-we-cannot-go-and-still-remain-who-we-thought-we-were.

This is death, as far as we know.

We've heard that we're all ascending a mountain of death, walking higher, daily, into the airless void that is incompatible with living. We can't *know* it yet, but we've heard this from everyone who has gone before us.

Sea level, and the womb from whence we began, is ever dwindling beneath us. The longer we continue our climbing march, the more debilitating our physical condition becomes and the more we become used to it; we carry this familiar burden. We limp, then crawl, then lie, gasping.

Philosophers and mystics ponder existence. Persistent, honest, driven and lucky ones push themselves into the vacuum of space and experience the breathless altitude beyond concepts of breathing or of "height," where all vestiges of atmosphere are fading wisps, below.

Returning to air once again, they use words such as "All" or "One." We thick-air breathers misinterpret their meaning; we misunderstand—but we get a feeling.

Life feels like something, right? It must be something.

This climber, this philosopher, the cancer survivor, that MS sufferer, all come back down to a place populated by distractedly-healthy people—the untouched-for-now.

Blindsided is the name of the book I'm reading about one man's reactions to his debilitating affliction.

Because aging is so slow, we miss the fact of its occurrence, except while at family reunions, where we see its work on others.

Before we leave, you must understand the lucky ones are <u>not</u> those who are blissfully unaware of their impending doom or Fate or destiny. The lucky ones have come nearest to their final selves, their real self, by reaching the thinness of no-air. They have returned in spite of the tremendous odds against their doing so—to appreciate the value, like never before possible, of their every in- and out-breath.

*

And what of that relentless presence, that sharp-bladed guillotine hovering over your head and mine?

On vacation, in traffic, at work, on a walk or while sitting—this blade remains our only true loyal lifelong companion. When we're with our pets, our kids, our spouses. Even on the edge of a mist-shrouded lake with the still water reflecting our image back to us. It is there.

All the more reason to serve and to offer up ourselves every moment we find ourselves within

THIS.

Yes. _This_ moment, too. We're a hundred feet higher on the mountain than before we started on this chapter. We have a better view; things seem even simpler and make more sense.

This is _our_ time. Now.

Please say, "Yes."

My blade is somewhat lower, I notice.

Oh, yes.

Chapter 16 — Short Story #1

Wind-swept eddies of snow swirling, spiraling and brushing across the frozen surface. Flowing through surrounding pines, the winds made an eternal sound. The man stood in his own footprints by the edge of the pond. Gloved hands. Knit hat. Scarf pulled over his nose. Snow pants over insulated boots.

His breath steamed away in the frigid air, taken by a shifting wind. Deer tracks. Flitting, small brown birds in the brush along the base of a drop-off leading to the pond.

Where? he wondered.

Patience.

After moments of concern over finding and not finding; obsessing over it being too late; and hoping it wouldn't be too late... he let it go—all of it. The wind still blew. What blows the wind? What pushes the pusher? It never matters. Nothing is important, he knows.

Stillness.

He settled into a heavy place within himself and lifted a foot, placing it into fresh, unmarked snow. He walked out onto the pond's lid of ice. The air sparkled when the sun caught flakes of tumbling, floating brilliance that twinkled like butterflies or miniature gold coins. He moved faster, and his feet began to sink beneath the visible ice surface.

Behind him, a trail of footprints blew itself slowly out like a frozen candle.

He took the invisible stairway down into the ice-covered pond. The surface of the ice reached his neck and then quickly disappeared overhead. He placed his feet onto each unseen step as complete blackness enfolded him in its embrace.

There was no feeling of being off-balance or of being tentative with his foot placement. He saw nothing and heard nothing.

In time, his motions, he realized, were those of a man walking on a level surface. He took another step and stopped. He was neither cold, nor hot. Nor anything. There was stillness and a muffled silence.

With eyes closed, he focused on the regular pulse he felt in his head and ears. His breathing was inaudible, and yet his chest expanded and his stomach moved with each breath. He felt encased within a muted clockwork. Pressure beneath his feet was all he knew of any external reality. He intended to stomp his right foot, and suspected that he felt its soundless impact. He stomped three times. His heel stung distantly.

Suddenly—*there.*

On what should be a floor was a long, thin line of brightness; a terminator. He had been clenching his eyes shut and yet, had still seen this light. When he slowly opened his eyelids, the line grew wider and taller.

The darkness retreated above and behind and became an opening orb, a spaceman's glare shield opening to light. He opened his eyes fully. Now he was immersed in a fuzzy whiteness; its contrast to total darkness was complete. Although there were still no sounds, it seemed as though his earplugs had been removed; the silence was no longer... muted.

He turned his gaze in a circle. Detecting no difference in the brilliant, fuzzy whiteness, he started walking. Like always.

The sensation of a supporting, hazy pressure was gone as well. Alone in this bright blur, he inhaled and was shocked to hear a long, drawn-in breath. He pursed his lips and blew, hearing a rush of air leaving his mouth and feeling his chest and stomach contract. He reached out to his sides, arms wide, and wiggled fingers, rotating hands. He waved his arms overhead, crazily, and jumped up and down.

Motion! Sensation! Perception!

He stopped moving and stood still. Breathing. He said, "Home, please."

He breathed in through his nose, and out through his mouth. He laid down on the white, hazy surface, rolling onto his back. It was somewhat cold. He stretched his arms and legs out and lay with closed eyes.

"Home is where the heart is," he whispered,

….awaking in a white room with bare walls and a very low ceiling. No door, no windows. Everything was white. He was lying on a square padded platform. Diffuse light filtered from the low ceiling onto him like a mist. He yawned and looked around, moving only his eyes.

Walls, ceiling, floor, nothing.

He strained to touch his chin to his chest. He appeared naked, although he was clothed, he knew, in a thin film neither visible nor touchable.

The man sat up and swung his legs over the side of the bed, propping himself up on his elbow before sitting upright.

Why did here exist? Who made it? Where was he? Each time he awoke here, he noticed himself asking questions such as these.

Eventually, it came to: *What am I looking for?* The unspoken reply was an itch that he couldn't scratch. A memory so close to consciousness that it was maddening.

He *knew* it was important, but... somehow, straining always blocked the door he was seeking to open.

Aaah.... That fine line of surrender. That tightrope.

He stood next to the bed, clothed in his transparent covering. He felt himself letting go. It was always a letting go—of hope, of caring. There was a membrane of fear and hungry anticipation. Each time he had to arrive honestly at honesty. *Each time*. There were no shortcuts or tricks or "ways around" it. Each time he had to be this way.

He dropped to the floor. The cold, hard surface smacked his face, settled on his cheek. His eyes closed and he felt the wind again, frigid on the melted snow on the exposed side of his face.

Sschhh-sschhhhaa of frozen particles blowing like sand past his hooded head. His breath steamed. His nose stung. His opened eye watered. His left cheek and hands, in contact with the ice, were beyond numb. He rolled from his belly onto his side, stiffly. He was an old man in the shadow of a twenty-year-old memory.

Struggling, he worked his way to hands and knees like a child, triceps trembling. Following a long-forgotten pattern, he slowly stood, hands on thighs, before straightening. He stood, once again on the pond.

He faced where he had come from, looking at the now unmarked snow to where he had stood on the shore before, ten feet away from the pond's edge. The gap seemed like a million miles.

Swaying, heartbeat slowing again, knees aching, numb hands held tightly against trembling thighs, he that knew fish were swimming ten feet beneath him.

Something in his neck ached when he tried to straighten. *Of course*, he ruefully thought.

He was cracking, like a thick glacial icepack steadily breaking down and growing thinner. Soon he would be in pieces, bobbing in the frigid ocean before melting into the comment-less depths.

Come on.

The silent words prompted him to move. Each day was different, but the same, in a way, and he always wondered, "What is the point?" He was familiar with this trend of his mind, and was no longer bothered when the question appeared.

There was no doubt this was what he was supposed to be doing. He would have liked to ask, "Why?" over and over and over. Not for an answer, not really. *Still.*

There *was*…. There was….

Beating his gloved hands against his legs, he winced as a pain shot down the left side of his neck. He took measured, crunching steps, following his disappearing tracks back into the snow.

Behind him, the wind and snow worked, brushing at the outlines of his boot prints on the frozen pond.

Chapter 17 — <u>#3</u>

All I've got are....
Maybe it....
"No," he said.

Silence is the backdrop.

No actor stands on the stage to deliver memorized lines. A man is lying in a reflective pool of blood. The blood has poured from his body like a vase of blood tipping over, pouring onto the wooden floor. The empty vessel lies on its side, hands motionless, head resting on one arm, outstretched legs like parallel logs.

The empty man laying on the stage. No audience witnesses his silent repose.

Here.

"The show *must* go on."

But this *is* the show.

His body, cold now, used to be warm; he had lived every moment of his life warm.

This lighting is familiar. It is focused on the nearly supine figure: stage front, mid. Bright spotlights converge, causing the surface of the body to remain slightly warmer than the darkened theater.

Congealing blood is confined by its hardening edges. Blood has sunk into and through gaps in the gritted black-painted hardwood flooring. Four small puddles contrast their rich, reflective, deepening color to the dusty concrete subfloor beneath the thin joists that support the actors' acting surface. Wet-seeming strands dangle motionless in this four-inch gap. Drops no longer connect the seen and unseen floors.

On stage: a heavy crimson curtain hangs on both sides of the performance area. Their folds are the color of darkened, dried blood. A black curtain hangs behind the acting space on the last of four parallel lines.

Empty stage: Except for the man lying in blood. Converged spotlights. Rows of empty seats in a darkened theater.

Perfect.

The man sits.

Caked blood coats the left side of his head and face. His movements were soundless. His hair is matted over the saucer-shaped indent where his skull is crushed.

Fresh lines of blood run along his jaw and drip from his chin onto a white pleated shirt beneath his dinner jacket. His arms remain locked at the elbows. His hands, on either side and slightly behind him, are propping him upright.

Perfect.

Legs, straight in front of him, end with polished black patent leather shoes over black silk socks covering ankles and shins. Shoestrings are tied perfectly. He listens. He blinks slowly. Very slowly. His left eyelid sticks and reopens. He notices the empty theater.

So. I am alone….

The sensation of being still….

Ah….

The man's head remains still. His eyes revolve in their sockets, left, then right. They track the silent rows of seats in the darkness, then point upward at the brilliant spotlights. Then, left and right again, across the unlit colored lenses and track lights.

His eyes settle downward to focus on his nose. The left side of his face is visibly darker. Eyes roll downward as far as possible, taking in motionless legs, feet, and a large region of pooled blood near his left hip. His orbs return to staring straight forward.

His eyelids slowly lower again to cover his eyes. He takes his first breath.

His left nostril remains clear. All of the inhaled air enters and then exits, no warmer than it had been while in the room.

Breathing continues.

Impossible, he thinks.

His heart is still. Staring at nothing behind the curtain of his eyelids, he wonders. *Will I stand, or lie back down*?

Chapter 18 — Friendship

[trente juillet deux mille treize]

Friendship.

Alone on an ocean-going vessel. Preferably alone... most of the time.

Here.

I'm in my boat, on this ship and I want it just right.

The right sunset to stare at for as long as I want; the right stateroom with the right breeze blowing in through those open portholes; the right rocking motion to this boat; the right seagulls with their sounds and that *certainty* of the water splashing and rushing as the ship cuts through the open ocean waves. My boat.

I want it just like this. No compromise.

Sitting on the deck, on the portside promenade, in the shade, reading a good book, and the day is perfect; I don't want you or anyone sitting down next to me, bothering me, distracting me from my book or this perfect setting, nor, taking *my* time reserved for contemplation, for staring into the distance, for letting my eyes wander along the horizon or along this projected metal bulkhead over me, to follow a wire conduit, or to idly trace the piping diverting storm runoff from the decks above.

I want to be alone. This is *my* boat. I have a limited time on this trip; it's not forever and it's getting closer to the destination. Luckily, I still can't see the shore. So, I don't want to waste any of my time listening to you talk about something I don't care about.

My boat.

I suppose everyone has the right to feel this. I feel this way.

The longer I spend on this ship, the more selfishly I guard my free time. I know how I want things around me to be.

"Free time" is not free; I have paid a fortune I couldn't afford to be here.

I'd rather just be silent. Except for now. Now, I'm leaning back in this chair, hands behind my head, or

I'm writing. Am I writing, now? Yes. Sure. I'm writing because you're listening.

You're me.

I don't worry about offending you, or having to justify my selfish time-keeping. Around you, I am able to be myself without much artifice. I care about you; I think of you as my friend; I am not as harsh with you, naturally, as I am with myself. I respect your... value.

When I see you at a table in the dining room I gladly join you and you don't seem to mind, although it never occurs to me to ask. If we meet on deck, walking our separate ways, I say "hi," with a smile.

At a bar—that one where there aren't too many people and the barkeep is just ordinary—on the middle deck, I buy you a cognac or a beer in the afternoon. I don't keep track. I buy you a drink because I want to.

When there's a problem below decks, like that one time, I'm there with a pipe wrench, sweating in the boiler room, straining to hold my end of a steam fitting repair job. The grease stays under my fingernails for a day or two afterward. The day after working there, I find my reclining seat on the deck again and pick up my book from the table.

When I see a good movie, I tell you. Sometimes you've already seen it. Sometimes you haven't, and you say you will.

I keep to myself for a *long* time. There are times when I've forgotten all about you. I deal with an illness or a minor injury or a problem I'm working on. Then I see you again in the hallway.

"Hey!" I say, "Long time!"

You're on your way somewhere. I am, too. We talk. It's good to run into each other. It's nice to say hi. It's always nice.

Last night, during that big storm, we were on the upper deck and found refuge from the torrential rain and wind in the pilothouse. The captain let us in there. The boat was turned uphill, into the waves, and the steepness as we went over another monster was frightening. The drop and banging of the ship going down the back of the waves was startling. It seemed like the ship would break in half. It was a relief every time.

It seemed like we wouldn't make it through the night.

This morning, seeing all that broken stuff on the ship was sobering. I didn't want to be sober. When we met at the bar, we raised our brandies.

You are my friend.

I can say "bye" without concern.

I wish you well.

Chapter 19 — Eternal Burgers

Bacon cheddar burgers on aluminum foil grilling in their own juices.

Smoke pours from under the edges of the grill when the grease on the foil runs through a hole or out the corner of the foil to drip onto the coals below. This smell is heaven. My ancestors from a million years ago nod in agreement at their own fires.

Sitting on a blue fabric chair, the kind that folds up and goes into a carrying case, I lean back and cross my left leg over my right knee. My non-smart prepaid Tracfone has a clock that I check. I have five minutes before I flip these six burgers. The lid is down.

I'm sitting on the concrete driveway at the corner of my front porch where the grill sits. It's summer.

A full glass of inexpensive Merlot sits on top of the rusted left side of a metal-lidded burner pad, next to a wire brush that I don't use anymore since I started using aluminum foil to grill. I take a sip, then a second. I lean the lawn chair back on two legs and inhale deeply through my nose and let it out with an *Aaaaah*.

I've backed our Pontiac family van a few yards closer to the road end of the driveway to have more room to sit in front of the grill. I've dragged the grill two feet away from the white vinyl siding-covered lower edge of our open front porch.

Two Christmases ago, I hung these big bulb colored lights up there where they're attached to the gutter along the front of our wide front porch, as well as along the guttered narrower sides of this covered porch. In the branches of the cherry tree on the other side of the porch, too.

Balanced on the back chair legs, I enjoy the humid night air and the smells—especially the smells—and look at the faded colored bulbs. Some of them, most of them, are showing more white light than colored because the color has worn off and flaked away and dried off in the heat and cold and sunlight over these past two years. They're still very nice. It's a very, very nice feeling, right here.

Mike, our large, hairy, white English Labrador with the shape of a polar bear and the heart of a sensitive kitten, lies on the concrete in front of my feet, in front of the grill. He's always nearest the source of food smells. He looks bored. He isn't. It's an act.

Two minutes.

Smoke is really rolling out now from the edges and holes in the closed grill that we inherited when we bought this place. The thermostat is edging up from "med" to "med-high." I lean forward to turn the dials on both burners down.

This *is* the life. You'll never hear me say differently.

Each time is ten minutes. Ten eternal minutes.

Thirteen or fourteen minutes altogether, today, however, because I started these six patties frozen and there's only one hot spot—one place on the grill that heats up well—and I need to shift the well-cooked and lesser-cooked burgers around when I turn them over, giving each their few minutes in the sunny spot. Still; ten minutes of eternity isn't bad. Give or take.

A snapshot of perfection:

There's always a couple stretches of three or four minutes within this time when everything is perfect.

That's what I like about these times at the grill— the frozen snowflake moments of smoky-punctuated perfection.

AND:

Mike, laying with head on paws and eyes closed; billowing burger smells in the humid, late-summer darkening air; the folding chair I got for father's day to watch Gui, my oldest, play soccer; the big, colored Christmas bulbs lending their warm glow; the first planets and stars of the early night sky; the lowering level in my glass and a fuzzy growing contentment.

Perfect.

Brief.

Eternal.

Other perfect moments at this rusting grill have witnessed Gui and his brother Ben playing football in our small front yard.

"Set—hike!"

Running, grappling, leaping over a red wagon with missing rubber on its back wheels; falling and laughing, shouting and grabbing—and then they're past the tall bushes where I can't see them. That's where all the exciting stuff happens, in front of the end zone, where the broadside of my work van parked just beyond the cherry tree by the front corner of our house forms the boundary.

"Touch down!"

This time, alone with Mike, I stand and reach for the tongs and take a final gulp of warm wine before setting the empty glass by the wire brush.

My phone alarm just sounded.

I lift the lid on the grill and revel in the sizzling heat and smoke.

Chapter 20 — Backflips

Off a diving board, backflips were always the easiest for me because from the beginning I could spot the landing almost the whole time and even if I did mess up I'd typically land feet-first, instead of on my back.

The first time I ever did a backflip was in 1990, in knee-high water on the beach in Tampa, while playing Frisbee with a friend. I was twenty-three. That first time, I looked over my left shoulder and kind of did a sideways flip, like you do in a bouncy-house when you're worried about the landing and you're trying to spot the landing the whole time.

My first time going straight back with my head— instead of looking over my shoulder—was <u>very</u> scary. This is the blind faith portion. The result, though, felt amazing. Going up-and-over and landing on my hands and knees in the warm, shallow, salty water, I was elated. Thrilled. It was totally unplanned. I had attempted a backflip on a whim. And then did five or six more. It was great. "Hey, Mark! Check this out!" I yelled.

I was there to sell my motorcycle to Mark, a fellow Florida Army National Guardsman. We were in the same combat engineering platoon in Lake City, where I lived. I had ridden my Honda Nighthawk 550cc down from Lake City, which is situated in the north central portion of the state. I took a Greyhound bus back north from Tampa.

Frontflips are blind finishing jumps; you just have to hope you don't under-rotate and land on your back, or over-rotate and smack your face on the surface. Backflips are easy to spot after that first blind beginning. Frontflips aren't.

At the beginning of the current summer, twice as old, twenty-three years after a sunny afternoon in shallow beach water in Tampa, I stood on the end of the diving board at the Wheeling, West Virginia public pool. I was forty-six. I turned around, facing backwards, crouched down, threw my hands upward and sprang up and back. I tucked my legs slightly. The shock of the cold water as I entered feet-first was familiar. First backflip of the summer.

I followed this with a back dive, then another backflip, and then a frontflip. These were my go-to tricks from the year before. Diving as high as possible was also something I could comfortably "go to." Jumping high above the end of the board, landing and springing up as high as I could possibly reach while diving straight into the sky, and then, reluctantly, turning to point downward once again, head-first, when gravity stops letting me go any higher. I eventually enter the water straight and clean.

Later, at the St. Clairsville, Ohio public pool, "Allen Pool" (maybe later in the week), I was diving, and there was a young boy who could do a pretty good frontflip. Really good, actually. He was maybe ten years old. I thought he could do a one-and-a-half, and I told him so. This is doing a frontflip with an extra half rotation, and the entry is a head-first dive instead of a feet-first landing. I told the boy that I always wanted to try one of those. He looked at me thoughtfully; I knew that look. "Be careful," I said. He tried the one-and-a-half at his next time at the board.

He tried it, and did a pretty good job; he wasn't *too* out of shape. By his third attempt, he'd *done* it. Nine or ten years old... wow. I thought, *The least I can do is try it once, since I encouraged* him *to do something in that unknown place of fearful-things-not-yet-tried.*

Unavoidable.

The one-and-a-half is something that I'd seen people do and always wished I could do. It always seemed so scary. Too scary. It didn't seem likely that I would ever attempt one. And yet.

"Well," I said, "I'm gonna try it, I guess."

Heart thumping, I ran, bounced on the end of the board as hard as I could, jumped as high as I could, and sort of froze-tucked while I tumbled forward. I landed face-smack-first during the spinning rotation into the slapping water. It was like hitting a sidewalk with my head whipping downward in a spin. In my deer-in-the-headlights mental freeze, I simply had no air-awareness; I had jumped, tucked, and head-spaced and *smacked,* head first. "Head-spaced" means that I froze, mentally. I hadn't managed to get my hands out.

Before this first attempt, I would see someone doing a one-and-a-half and feel *very* envious watching them do something I knew I would never attempt; it was just too dangerous and I was too old to do it without getting hurt.

This first try hurt! And it was *glorious.* I knew right away what I'd done wrong and what I had to do more of next time. Anticipatory fear was mostly replaced by excitement and a newfound healthy respect for that head-smacking landing. The trick, I knew, was getting your hands out in front of you because that forward spinning adds an exponential amount of torque to any surface strike; it was like diving head-first with no hands to part the water.

I tried it about nine more times that day. Even now, I can feel the hard concrete smack on the top of my head. The top of my head was *sore.* In successive visits to the pool throughout the summer, after many dozens of attempts, I realized that I hadn't been projecting my spin *upward* like I should have; I'd been pulling that tight spinning inward; basically projecting the torque downward, which didn't give me much time to spot the landing, or to get my arms alongside my head and straighten out.

Eventually, I figured this all out, and my entries into the water were straight and unhurried; I had plenty of time to get situated because my rotations happened higher above the surface.

Back to that first one-and-a-half day at Allen Pool: I had a headache from hitting the water hard with the top of my head. Oh, joyful pain! The last few times, that first day, I'd rotated around, extended my hands and entered the water looking somewhat like I was diving. Andrée told me that the last ones actually looked pretty good. How great it feels to go home with that accomplishment filling my heart. I won't try to tell you what I mean, but I hope that you already know, or will find out yourself one day, doing something, anything, you'd always hoped to do.

*

It took me two more pools—visits to the Wheeling Park pool and then, to the Barnesville public pool, before I "got" it. This one-and-a-half is still something I consciously remind myself to jump high enough for, projecting upward instead of forward; and I tell myself to tuck enough, and to straighten out with my hands. I never assume that I don't need to hear this. Still, I can always pull one out of the hat that looks respectably impressive.

After each of those summer "Diving Days of Improvement," I felt awesome. Just fabulous. I lay in bed each night afterward, replaying dives I'd done.

Bliss.

My next new thing was an inward-facing pike dive.

An older man than me—probably in his fifties—had stood on the end of the board at the Wheeling pool, facing inward. I wondered what he was going to do. A backflip? I walked along the pool's edge, watching. He put his hands high overhead, then exploded upward and backwards, folding at the waist, and then dove straight in. Man, did that look cool! It also looked impressively difficult, but at the same time, there weren't any spinning or scary twisting parts to the dive, and I had a strong feeling that I could do it, too.

I can do that. This means that I felt the reassuring certainty that it was within my limited range of capability. I had a feeling—and I assume that most people do—for what kinds of things I can attempt successfully. For me, this meant mainly non-twisting moves that weren't too difficult and didn't involve more than one rotation. The inward-facing pike looked reassuringly, excitingly, like something I could do. Besides, it was cool-looking! There weren't even any blind times where I wouldn't be able to see the water.

I stood on the end of the springboard facing the edge of the pool, jumped up and back, hunched my back in an awkward "C" shape, and face planted sideways, slapping my side on the water, landing very off-balance and painfully. My second time was worse, and hurt even more.

Then I saw that guy. He must have felt bad for me. Without my having to ask, he said, "You have to stick your butt up when you go up and back. I jumped off to the side when I was starting."

That was the biggest potential problem with this one, I thought—hitting my face on the diving board if I didn't project back far enough. My two first attempts must have looked like I had the potential of hitting head-first on the board.

With the reminder to myself to stick my butt up in the air, my next jump was actually better. "Better" means it hurt less. I still landed somewhat on my side and awkwardly, but this time I entered the water head-first, with arms out, although still somewhat protectively folded-up. Climbing the ladder after this jump, I was grinning. I thanked the man.

"You'll get it," he said, walking away. Three more times, and I landed my first inward-facing pike.

Man!

As before, I re-played those successful dives in my head while driving home and while lying in bed that night before sleeping.

I was absolutely thrilled. Completely elated. I felt alive and great. What's the big deal with jumping into a pool? I can't explain it. If you wonder, I'll just say that I can't give you an answer that makes sense. Maybe if we were talking…. Show me somebody who likes jumping in the water, or who likes doing anything for the thrill of it, and our shared grin when one of us, or the other, tries something for the first time—and then perfects it—will communicate precisely what is involved with the urge to push into untried, new things.

I was thrilled. Each time, at one of the three area pools, there was a definite progression of development in this meaningless activity.

*

Through a fabulous world of discovery, I'd do new tricks, sometimes two or three never-before-tried moves in one day. Someone else would always be around, jumping or diving, too. Someone else doing something that I hadn't done yet, or that I couldn't imagine doing yet. Similar souls.

My next trick was one I came up with on my own: a gainer dive. I'd had it in my head that it *must* be possible to stand at the end of the diving board, facing forward, and spring up and do a backflip-type move that ends with a straight head-first dive into the water below the board. I never saw anyone else trying this at the pools I went to, but I was certain that divers *must* do it if I could think of it! I had the mental image of this forward-facing backwards landing dive, and it felt like it did when I first saw the guy doing his pike dive. *I can do this....*

The next time I went to the pool in Wheeling Park, I tried it off the springboards. I landed flat on my back, of course, and terribly off-balance. It hurt like hell. The second time hurt even more, and felt worse. There's a lifeguard perch on the right side of those two diving springboards. I asked the young guard sitting there what he thought I was doing wrong, or, what I could do differently.

"You're almost there," he said. "Throw your hands back more."

Amazingly, that was all it took—just a little unexpected encouragement and throwing my hands back more.

I went for it again, throwing my hands and head back in earnest, while jumping up from a standing position at the end of the board and arching my back while going backwards. Just like that first going-straight-back backflip. Scary-blind.

Weirdly, I found myself watching an upside-down world and the diving board I'd just left, and the people standing in line behind the diving board—all moving upward in slow motion as I dropped straight down. My biggest fear had been hitting the board with my face while arching backward.

The lifeguard shook his head dismissively. "No, you're way far away from the board." I thanked him for his advice.

With a tremendous feeling of relief at not hitting the board with my face, I stood up there again, flexed my knees, and simultaneously pushed up while throwing my hands back with my arms alongside my ears, palms linked together with my head tipping back, while spotting my landing. Legs straight. Back arched. Once again, the disconcerting feeling as I arched up and back and down in a big slow arc. I entered the water like an arrow.

Whew!

Now I had a handful of new and even cooler-looking tricks that I could work through each time I came to the pool. The rest of that day, and during following visits to the area pools in the summer's sweltering heat, I practiced, over and over, including all of my other "standard" moves into the rotation—backflips, frontflips, back dive, front high dive. I had a long, long terrific blast of a time every day of swimming. Maybe once a week we went. Sometimes twice a week. Sometimes every other week.

Each post-diving evening, I was deeply, comfortably fatigued. Often, the next day, I would have a sore neck, or a sore lower back, or something else would be tweaked, but the sheer joy and satisfaction I felt upon replaying those dives and jumps in my mind was pure ambrosia and balm. I considered this pain a very small—and appropriate—price to pay for such joy.

*

Barnesville has a high dive and a lower diving board. It's the only high diving springboard in the three local outdoor public pools I visit. The lower board's surface is about five feet above the water. The high diving board is 12 to 15 feet above the water. At first, I could only do a _very_ tentative headfirst dive from up there. That thing is high! _Very_ scary. Also, the bottom of the pool in Barnesville slopes rapidly shallower, and when I dove too far out the first time, my hands hit the rising surface.

I was _much_ too afraid to do a frontflip or a backflip from up that high. I'd seen younger guys doing them, but it wouldn't be me, I felt. I was quite afraid. Yet.... I _could_ do a one-and-a-half, and a gainer, and an inward facing pike dive from the lower springboard. I _should_ be able to do _something_ from up there, right?....

Feeling very afraid, I first did my most comfortable non-dive from the high dive—a backflip. It went shockingly, surprisingly, well. It was easy.

I had thought that I would over-rotate and die. Instead, I soared through the air slowly, easily, and landed feet-first. There was _so_ much time to spot the landing! I'd had nightmare visions of various bad endings. Nope. In fact, the sheer time I had in the air was an unexpected gift. Before, I'd only focused on the dying; now, I had much more time to spot my landings.

Then, the frontflip. This one scared me even more than my old standard backflip. I didn't want to under- or over-rotate and land on my back or on my face. Before the first jump, my companion was that paralyzing fear that I always felt before attempting something unknown. The fear of that first unknown equals, basically, paralysis. I could not afford to take a half or a tentative step, however; this would very likely hurt me more than a wholehearted, failed attempt. A first attempt equals the first real <u>data</u>: *Now I've got something to work with*. It doesn't matter how badly or well the attempt goes. *Now I know something* is always the result.

Well, I did it.

Of course, like with my other tricks, I did the frontflip and my other moves from the high dive over and over; getting the timing right and hitting the water dozens of times. <u>Easily</u> dozens. Having more air time means I could fold my hands and extend my arms alongside my ears for pain-free head-first entries.

Down on the lower board, I practiced my one-and-a-half again and again and again and again; I won't say how many times. Fine-tuning, bouncing higher, throwing my hands forward more forcefully, tucking tighter, getting my arms straightened alongside my ears with overlapped hands—all of these adjustments made to tweak each dive until it felt perfect. Out of ten dives, two or three would be unquestionably perfect. To be "perfect" means effortless, with no pain from hitting the surface. Everything feels *right*.

On the lower board, still, I worked on the inward facing pike and my new, favorite scary move, the backward arching gainer dive, which, every time I did it, I assumed I'd hit the board with my face, and yet, with astonishment, would instead watch the board rising above me in slow-motion as I entered the water.

With my successes of the frontflip and backflip off the high dive—that high, high, scary diving board—I decided to try my other moves up high there too, the very next time I visited the Barnesville pool with my family.

Oh. Yes. I *was* at these swimming pools every time with my family; with my sons and my wife. This was one of our family summer activities—my obsessive jumping being the added, expected, ever-present ingredient. I <u>do</u> realize that I haven't mentioned my family yet.

I'd say to my wife on the way to the board, "Andrée, watch this one," as I was about to do something untried, or a new twist on an old trick I'd thought of attempting.

Gui and Ben would be at the pool, too, doing their own jumps. Much of the time they preferred to swim in the larger pool, playing "Marco Polo" or tag with their mom and friends. I would join them there on occasion, but really, the siren song of the diving boards would lure me away with another idea to try.

*

The following week's visit to the Barnesville swimming pool high springboard dive:

Back dive.

Standing on the end of the board, facing inward, I interlock my palms over my head, arms alongside of my ears. I spring gently upward and backward, arcing, eventually hitting the water straight, hands first. Very, very scary, but really simple. As well as impressive-looking. Andrée said this is one of her favorite dives. The first time from up high, I over-leaned and smacked my thighs off the water, on my way toward a belly flop. *Ouch.* I was thrilled. I actually landed hands-first, which I always attempt to do on a head-first dive.

Inward-facing pike dive.

This one felt much less scary because there was no blind time when I couldn't see the landing, but... again, it was quite frightening... that's a <u>long</u> drop.

"It should work; it's the same thing," I muttered to myself, as well as to the attendant lifeguard sitting off to the side; I'd hoped that she would be ready to rescue me if I did something dumb and lost consciousness after a disastrous fall.

The way of diving that doesn't hurt my head: I "discovered" it two years before this high diving day. Two years earlier, I had the after-image in my mind of watching Olympic divers on TV, and felt curious about how they managed to dive from a 30-foot platform without concussing themselves on the surface of the water with every entry into the concrete liquid.

I wondered about this because I had a very clear memory of diving from that same approximate height—once—many years before.

It was a crystal-clear water spring hole on a sweltering, baking afternoon near the town of Live Oak, in the northern panhandle of Florida. My brother and I had ridden our motorcycles down a long sandy lane to find a group of people jumping in, diving into, swinging over and dropping into and swimming through a liquid oasis. From fifty feet away, you wouldn't have known there was anything except more scrub oaks, pine trees and Spanish moss as far as the eye couldn't see. From the edge of the sinkhole, though, there was an amazing crater, three hundred feet across, that dropped straight down from the surrounding land. A limestone sinkhole with deep, dark, cold, amazingly clear water.

Its extensive caves attracted divers, alligator-like goggled heads bobbed in a group on the murkier edge of the spring hole. On the opposite edge, someone had nailed steps and three levels of tiny platforms on two Cypress trees leaning over the water's edge. I dove once from the second-highest, from around thirty feet up. I didn't know about the hands then.

I thought I had broken my skull. I shouldn't have dived in. I was grateful that I hadn't broken my head open like an egg, or lost consciousness under the dark cold water; at first, I was certain I had cracked my head open, when I reached the shore, I was surprised to feel with my fingers that I hadn't.

Back to my Olympic memories: I watched, as everyone watches when the commentators critique the dives, those slow-motion replays. I saw that the divers' hands were curiously overlapped at the ends of their straightened arms. Overlapping, aligned palms. Thumbs interlocked. Arms alongside ears. They hit the water palms first!

At a pool in New York, I tried this strange way of holding my hands. Wow! It didn't hurt. I entered the water as smoothly as silk. *Strange....*

That time, my family was visiting various public pools during our summer on a horse farm outside of Binghamton, New York.

The high dives I did two years later, on the second high-dive day in Barnesville's pool, didn't hurt either. When I was a kid, I used to dive with my arms outstretched but separated, and every time my head would take the impact of the water.

Moving on. From the high dive, without *that* head-smacking punishment, I worked on eliminating other sources of pain. I adjusted my entry angle and straightened my legs (when I was scared, I tended to go in with my legs bent—a fear-reaction—or I'd over-rotate and my legs would flop backwards over my head).

Okay:

Back dive.

Inward-facing pike dive.

Gainer dive.

Backflip.

Frontflip.

High, soaring dive.

Check, check, check, check, check and check. All of these done from that high diving springboard. On the lower one, I kept doing my one-and-a-half, as well as newer things like a sideways bouncing and then a backwards bouncing backflip—I ran on the diving board, jumped up, landing on the end of the board either sideways or backwards, to spring upward to do my backflip. The result was higher and better-looking than a standing backflip. It was to be the start of a new twist. More on that later.

Bailey, a boy who had played on the same rec. center soccer team the previous year with my older son, Guillaume, was doing very good frontflips. This was <u>his</u> go-to impressive-looking trick.

I told twelve-year-old Bailey that a backflip was much easier than the frontflips he was doing with ease.

Just a few minutes before, Benjamin, my younger son, had successfully attempted his own first backflip! I was so proud of him—not for his successfully doing one, but for his really going for it after a few initial false starts and half-attempts. I have <u>much</u> respect for people who do something it is hard to make themselves do.

It's a very scary thing—that first time you go for it; that fully-committed straight back thing with your head; most everyone looks over one shoulder while doing their first backflip. Some quit after one or two frightening, frozen, half-attempts and painful landings. To graduate to keeping one's head straight while going up-and-over backwards is the real sign of commitment; it's the next level.

After Ben's first backflip and repeated (!) backflips, Bailey stood at the end of the lower springboard several times, heels right on that fear barrier that we all know, so well. Thirty seconds would pass, and then he'd turn around, shaking his head, and walk back to the steps.

"No. I'm too scared," he'd say. I knew exactly what he felt. I also could see that he would easily do a backflip—if only he could "go for it" *just one time*.

"If you do your backflip," I said, pointing, "I'll do my one-and-a-half off that high dive." I couldn't believe I had just said this.

I was terrified at the prospect. In this sense, I was on Bailey's fear's side; I didn't want him to do his challenge, because I didn't want to have to do *mine*. Then again, the same as with that other boy who was facing a new trick, I felt that the least *I* could do was to put myself in the same scary position I was urging another into—to the point of doing something scary for the first time.

What is this "scary" I keep talking about? It is simply the feeling that you're going to die.

I didn't talk much after my commitment to Bailey. I didn't try to encourage him any further. I hoped that he wouldn't do his backflip because I felt more scared than eager to do my own challenge. Yet.... I must say that data and preparation *helps*. There's nothing like preparation and data, and I know it. I had a *lot* of preparation under my belt. I'd also accumulated some small quantity of data; I'd familiarized myself with this new height's drop by doing various other tricks dozens of times. I'd also practiced, over and over and over, both visualizing and actually doing my one-and-a-half from that lower board. Many, many, many times. Though I wasn't ready, I was ready.

As Bailey kept revisiting his own threshold of fear on the end of the board before walking back to the ladder, I practiced perfecting my one-and-a-half on the lower board. I *knew* I was going off the big tall springboard no matter what Bailey decided to do or not do. Unfortunately for me, I knew Bailey was going to live to swim another day. I, on the other hand, was going to do my trick, and would probably die.

I did all of my tricks one more time except for the one-and-a-half—all from the big board—trying to grow more and more comfortable with that tall place.

Finally, Bailey spoke aloud what I already knew. I'm sure he was disappointed and relieved at the same time. He didn't have quite enough data, I suspected, and his fear was still too big to get around. I think it's really best to <u>not</u> do something if you're held too tightly by the fear. Fear is <u>good</u>; it saves lives.

I called over to Andrée to get her iPhone because I was going to try my one-and-a-half from that high dive. I couldn't believe I said that. *Idiot!*

"I need you to document the disaster," I said.

Heart pounding, with an *oh, boy* feeling while standing at the top of the ladder on that tall, tall diving board, I said these two words aloud more than once: "Oh, boy." A few yellow jackets, whose nest was on the underside of the high diving board, hovered just to my left, below my feet.

I ran, jumped up and bounced on the end of the board with my arms above my head, I threw my hands downward as I was projected higher, I spun and tucked for that familiar period of time, and then opened back up to stop my rotation, with hands overlapped like those Olympic divers, my arms alongside my ears, and—

Splooosh.

I hit the surface and entered the water in an almost-dive. I smacked my thighs a bit as my legs were drawn slightly up in a quasi-protective crouch.

Oh, *boy.*

The relief at having tried it and survived! Unspeakable. The elation of succeeding. I hugged my wife and asked her, "You got that?" She assured me she had. Before too much time passed, I knew I had to ask her to get her phone camera ready again; the first time was fine, but I needed to hit the water in a better dive position, and not wait too long.

I did it again.

It was better; it felt better and it worked out better. I had more air-awareness (less fear-paralysis); I'd opened my eyes before hitting the surface, and actually straightened out my dive.

Absolutely. Incredible. There is no way. Even now, I can't believe I did all that stuff that summer. I'm 46 [and older now, of course]. Did I say that? It's not ancient, I know, but, *man.* I guess 46 is old enough to be mature enough to be brave enough to try things and to work on them progressively, methodically. Maybe. There's also a little courage. And the joy of exploration. The exhilaration of success. Persistence. And, I'm possibly not quite old enough to be too old to do some of the physically-demanding things that I did during this summer of diving.

After that, my other tricks, like everything I'd been doing, continued to develop and progress.

The last big thing I focused on attempting during that summer of diving was a double frontflip—a double front somersault. One day, near the end of summer at the Wheeling Pool, I tried it three or four times in a row. The next week, I attempted it two more times. Andrée said they looked okay. They hurt like hell.

The first day of attempts, I badly bruised the kidney area of my lower back. The second day these bruises, black and yellow by then, were smacked harder than I remember from the week before.

While rotating in a forward roll in the tucked position, as you hit the water, there are multiplied forces—both in the vertical drop and the spinning, torqued slapping into what feels like a concrete sidewalk after dropping from a two story building. It felt like I landed squarely on my curved back. I probably did. Everyone except me thought that I'd done a good trick.

No more, I swore silently, through the pain while crawling-swimming to the ladder at the side of the pool's diving area.

I had data now. It wasn't *all* about the anticipatory fear anymore. When I did the first double attempt, I just tucked and decided to keep spinning until I hit the water. Oh, boy. I hit it.

Andrée said that it looked fine but sounded really bad. My slapping water strike broadcast all the way to the top of the water slide three hundred feet up the hill from the pool. I walked slowly away from the water after my first attempt and sat down on a wooden bench where our towels, backpacks and shoes were scattered.

After the pain faded, believe it or not I moved on to my other tricks, perfecting them…. *No way* was I going to try that double again. Later, a passing lifeguard who had seen my first attempt told me I was nearly there. I wasn't a fan of failing. I got that familiar, whispered idea in my head to do it *just one more time*.

I bounced extra high, tucked tighter, and landed excruciatingly on my lower back again, on top of a cement automobile after falling twenty stories from a skyscraper that I'd foolishly decided to somersault from.

The sound I made as I hit the water was even louder than the first time. This was my second day of trying those doubles, and it was the last time I would do it that year. It would have been nice to have a trampoline and harness set to practice those spins.

Applause erupted from a second lifeguard sitting on his raised chair on the other side of the diving area; he told me it had looked great. Technically, in two days' visits, I had done four double front somersaults. And paid for them. *This* trick wasn't as enjoyable as the other things I'd tried that summer. I quietly suspected that I'd lacerated or ruptured internal organs.

*

Bruises from my second double frontflip attempt were less terrible-looking than the first time. Maybe my back was getting used to being smacked, or maybe the bruises were too tired to get all colored up again. Or maybe the bruising of my organs was too deep to be seen without an MRI. Maybe that area of my back was so traumatized that it wasn't capable of bruising anymore.

It turns out I would have one more day at the Wheeling pool where I would find myself effortlessly performing a category of tricks that I previously knew beyond a doubt I would never do. I know I've said that before. I hadn't assumed these were out of my reach; I <u>knew</u> they were.

This last swimming day of our summer, I felt a curious lassitude. Focus-less, I had no goal; there was no new trick on my "to do" list. Several times, I found myself standing on the end of the diving board with a completely blank mind. No thoughts of jumps or dives that I wanted to try. I didn't have any *wants*. Everything was in slow-motion, including me.

The sun was hot. It wasn't too warm, though. The pool was sparsely peopled; this was my favorite kind of day because lines for the waterslide and the diving boards were nonexistent. Perfect, by my standards.

Then I saw a young man in his early twenties perform an interesting frontflip. He had thrown in a 360-degree spin with this standard jump. It added an exciting twist to the movement and it looked great. He was rotating on two axes. This was a spinning frontflip.

I told him I was impressed and said I'd always admired those twisting jumps and had seen another guy earlier in the summer doing crazy big ones.

"How do you do it?" I asked, mildly curious, not intending to do anything with what he said.

This affable guy, twenty-plus years my junior, on my last swimming day of that summer, said, "You just roll your shoulder."

When he said this, I saw his demonstrating movement as he stood on that springboard. *Recognition*. Something clicked. I *knew* this. This is not a thinking thing. I knew that motion as soon as he did it because any good faller knows what to do when the ground is approaching quickly. I'd rolled a *lot* when I was obsessed with Karate in my twenties. I'd also rolled *quite* a bit in my thirties when I was obsessed with inline skating at skate parks on ramps and skating for hundreds of miles on trails, roads, parking lots and even down concrete stairs. I had a *lot* of practice falling.

Standing on the left-side diving board that had better traction, I told this friendly young man, "Okay, I'll try it."

What a change! Totally unplanned; none of my usual anxiety build-up before something new.

And how fun!

This rotating on another axis made the landings seem softer. Imagine that. Granted, I was only doing a familiar frontflip in a different way, but it felt *fun*.

After the first two times, I managed a hundred and eighty degree spinning front flip, landing in the water facing the diving board.

The nearby lifeguard, who had been watching, said, "Those look pretty good with a backflip."

Hmmm…. Say no more. The backflip was my favorite comfort move.

The thing with those spinning backflips, I found, is a tucking-under movement with my right shoulder; this is in line with my preferred direction to spin which, being left-handed, is counter-clockwise.

"This one looks *great*," Andrée told me, after I showed her the move. She took videos of these spinning frontflips and backflips. I haven't looked at them yet. Maybe they've been deleted from her phone by now. I always forget to ask.

I jumped each of these spinning moves a couple of dozen more times. They were fun. Rotating more each time, I was able to do three-hundred-and-sixty-degree spinning backflips and frontflips. *Imagine!* These maneuvers were something I'd never dreamed of trying—I know I always say it but this time I mean it—and here I was, doing them with ease.

I'd been feeling the Achilles tendon on the back of my left foot smarting a bit. Increasingly, I limped each time, carefully, from the ladder out of the pool to the diving board. Each time, I'd push off the diving board even harder than before and attempt to jump higher. By the time I left the pool that day I was *done*.

Hobbling to the car across the baking parking lot, and then from the car to the house, on up the stairs for my shower that night, and along the hall into our bedroom, both Achilles tendons were swollen and quite tender. I took Ibuprofen and put ice on the left one.

The following day, I hobbled around the house, noticing my calf muscles were sore. On reflection, it seems that I'd torn and strained a few things.

On the last day at the pool, in addition to all the jumping, I suspected, too, that walking up the asphalt path to the waterslide repeatedly hadn't helped, either.

Weeks later, my left Achilles was still tender when I'd run or carry something upstairs.

Today, I threw a football with Gui. I rode the zip line in our back yard a few times, hiking up the hill to the starting point. Both Achilles are a little sore. Yesterday, I was running around with Gui as he practiced at the Capstone Soccer Complex where his U-12 team plays.

I'm done with my summer of swimming and diving. It was one of those summers. I know it. I knew it when it was happening and I sure know it now. I was allowed this marvelous time in this recent late summer of my life.

I went to the chiropractor the week following that last swim day with a nagging stiff neck that didn't feel much better after his adjustments. Two weeks later, my neck was fine again and both calves and tendons are better.

Next year, I'll be 47 [already am now, as you've guessed]. I'm probably forty-seven now [I am]. My goal for next summer is to perfect that double front somersault, and to explore more of those dual-rotation spinning jumps.

With the one-and-a-half and the double front somersaults, I'm pretty sure that the thing is to jump up as I'm doing the spinning; what I'd *been* doing is focusing all of my attention on throwing my arms downward to kick-start the necessary spin, which hadn't helped me gain enough height to complete the rotations before hitting the water.

Live and learn.

You build on what you've done before. Complication-of-movement, progression of skill and increasing competence all grow together like a grand tree. Amazing, how we do things and how we learn. I wish I had known *this* world when I was twenty-seven or seventeen—or thirty-seven or seven. What could we *really* do if we knew?

Those last-days twisting flips were an unexpected gift. The right combination of fatigue, a helpful demonstration, a lack of focus and *voila*! Moves I'd never considered doing myself.

Without the usual fanfare of fear, I was doing tricks that I knew I couldn't do—doing them comfortably. I was in a perfect eye of a perfect summer storm, with no wind or passage of time and a clear sky under which these amazing-looking and amazing-seeming twisting somersaults and backflips occurred.

You never know what's going to happen.

I paid with those Achilles strains. I took fish oil pills. They seem to help. I think they're supposed to be good for connective tissue.

Thank you for allowing me to be here and for letting me do these things.

*

Coda:

In my forty-seventh year (is it forty-eighth, when you're forty-seven?), I had a minor swimming summer. I didn't do much in the way of new tricks. If anything, I seemed to backslide, not performing my tried-and-true movements with the usual expected grace and ease. Still, there were a couple of notable points from the more recent summer to mention.

At the Barnesville pool with its 12' high board, I did my one-and-a-half front somersault again— twice. I didn't land very prettily; on the second one I over-rotated and smacked into the liquid concrete in a line drawn between the tops of my shoulders. I just didn't have the reps in that year; I hadn't done the one-and-a-half very many times from *any* board, whereas the year before, I'd done this move dozens upon dozens of times on the lower board before trying it from up high. When I did it from up there this second year, I was out of the zone. Simply *attempting* those two from the high board I count as a personal significant milestone because of how scared I was to do them—and to *not* do them. I felt that a door on my being able to do these things was closing. Stronger than my fear of doing them again was my desire to do those one-and-a-half dives from up there, *this* year, before another year had come and gone. So I did them.

A second highpoint, which surprisingly didn't hurt much at all, was being able to do those three-sixty backflips and frontflips whenever I went to the Allen Pool in St. Clairsville or to the Barnesville pool. I could land them whenever I wanted to. My old standard tricks might have been off the menu, but I was able to serve up these newest tricks each time they were ordered. When I'd do them, all the people would stop and look. I worked on getting them up higher and higher. They're fun, and they feel great. There's a measured *whomp...--whomp...--whomp* feeling that I get during the stretch of time before landing in the water. The feeling of being pulled by centrifugal acceleration along two separate lines or axes is a unique sensation. Like those astronauts strapped, spread-eagle, into their spinning gyroscopic NASA disorientation machines. While doing a three-sixty backflip, I feel the *whomp...--whomp...--whomp* as my body experiences the intersection of two overlapping spinning circles. <u>What</u> a feeling. It seems like I hang in the air forever.

Well. We'll see what happens next year.

Chapter 21 — Tunnel

Water.

Still.
Moving.

Just a few seconds....

Time-sense. No sense.

No-time, no sense of time; no sense of talking to oneself about sense and time and meaning.

Only so many brain cells left. What are you going to do with them?

Only so much time for each one.

Only so long.

Only, only, only, only, only, only, only. Only.

A heart beats *with* time, *in* time:

Thub-thub;

Thub-thub.

A metronome in the head, in the pulsing carotid neck artery, seen in the pupils opening in time, each time to each pulse of blood in the closed eternal hula hoop of vital fluids circulating from beginning to end and back to begin again and again. A ceaseless, fleshly Monopoly game; always passing "Go," never stopping, never.

I saw a dead deer today while I was walking my dog in Schuler Park in Flushing. *Very* strong rotting odor. Its carcass was lying at the base of a tree. I wondered what had killed it. I wondered what had eaten into the ribcage like that. Coyotes? Wild dogs? Foxes? Skunks? Raccoons? Possums? Cats? Black birds? Vultures? Maggots and beetles? All of them?

Mike smelled the carrion, of course. He has a very active nose; he's a sniffer. He's got good eyes, too. I always thought dogs weren't supposed to have good eyes.... Maybe his eyes are good because his ears are bad. I walked quickly past the dead animal, keeping him far away by gently tugging on the retractable leash. He didn't show me that he minded avoiding the stinking carcass. Come to think of it, when you fart, dogs don't seem to notice or care, even when we know that they have a much more sensitive nose than we do. What smells *do* they find offensive?

*

"You're really a great guy, Dave," Keith says.

"I can't tell you how much I appreciate all you've done for me," he intones into my right ear.

I was propping my small cell phone between my shoulder and ear as I put the piece of paper with his number back in my pants pocket.

I'd just finished fixing his collapsed aluminum awning on the building he owns along US 40, west of Bridgeport, Ohio and east of Blaine Hill. His awning had collapsed in a wind storm last winter. It had looked increasingly awful ever since. I had lifted it from the concrete porch, installed new supports and hunted through the bushes in front of his building and alongside the empty lot next to his building for the interlocking aluminum slats that had fallen out and blown away.

I pop-riveted everything together, attaching new supports under the aluminum slat awning and screwing the frame to these supports. At the end of the porch, I trimmed back an evergreen bush that had grown into the awning and then called Keith from my work van when I was done. My four-ways were blinking and I sat in my '96 GMC Safari where I'd pulled over as far as I could onto the overgrown sidewalk around twenty feet before the end of Keith's building. This busy street is narrow, and cars and trucks blow by my left side-view mirror. I could reach out and touch them.

I told Keith we could settle up the next time he saw me. Some hardware, my time—I'd given him a break, but I wanted to be paid something for my time.

I don't think I'm going to collect. That was months ago. I saw him on the fourth floor of Wheeling Hospital today. He had a full beard and a freshly-stitched cut on his forehead, with an IV in the back of one hand and a large bandage on the same forearm. He was emaciated-looking and seemed to be calmly, vacantly, there; although I don't know if he was really *here*. He recognized me. After a while he got tired and I left. He sincerely thanked me for stopping by. He was markedly gracious.

A mutual friend told me that he and his wife had found Keith nearly dead a week earlier in another house (not the building with the awning), in the hills above the northeast end of Wheeling. Arnie said that the EMTs had come to pick Keith up. And now, Keith's in Wheeling Medical Park. The day after I saw him, Arnie said Keith had taken "a turn for the worse." I don't know what that means, except he was in ICU again, one floor below where he'd been when I visited him.

My understanding is that he had been delirious and hypothermic, suffering from exposure, crawling around largely unclothed, in his unheated shack of a building off a steep winding road in the West Virginia hills above Benwood, a somewhat run-down town on the north end of Wheeling. His "townhouse" building, where I fixed the awning, is across the Ohio River, just west of Bridgeport. Several old BMWs sit in the grass behind his place.

Bridgeport and Wheeling are directly across from one another on the state line, which is the Ohio River, here.

*

Don, another mutual acquaintance closer to Keith's age than I am, told me a week ago, "It's a real shame that he let himself go that way.... Someone so sharp, so talented and with so much potential. To do that to themselves...." Don shook his head. I got the impression that he'd seen this before. People with so much promise sliding down a chute, faster and faster, to nowhere.

I don't know what Keith did to himself or what he's still doing. The last I heard, he was in a continuous care facility. Arnie and Mary Ann said that he had drunk himself out of existence. That's my phrase to describe what they described. Some alcoholics eventually arrive in a kind of delirium state. Their mind gives out before their liver. I'd known Keith for around eight years, and I know enough to be certain that if anyone ever found out his whole story, it would make a movie life that actors would fight each other to portray.

Maybe Keith had done nothing other than what I'm doing to myself and what you're doing to yourself. We're all on a trajectory. Signs of addiction are rampant.

Addiction? What? Addiction to what?

—to moods and to feelings and to preferences and reactions such as disappointment, depression, hope, despair, shame and… simply, resolutely giving up.

Mary Ann said that, ironically, Keith was now very serene and happy. We all know him as someone who tended toward combative aggressiveness.

"Happy!" she said. "Imagine that."

*

Hi guys!

Last night's meeting was walking through the Wheeling Railroad Tunnel behind OVMC (Ohio Valley Medical Center) in northeast Wheeling.

The actual topic was "How we interact with the world."

A couple of hours before the meeting, I saw Keith, a friend of the group, at Wheeling hospital in room 471 of the new addition. He was admitted four days before. He seemed to be doing better. They're giving him fluids, rest and food.

How we interact with one another; how we banter, small talk, pause, and all of that; this became highlighted to me as I was visiting Keith. When we're alone with ourselves, we interact with our world, too. We talk to it, and to ourselves. I do, at least. We do things. We act. We pause. When we're chit-chatting or when we're silent in one another's company, I think this silence is at least more honest. I tried to be honest, and polite while visiting Keith.

It occurred to me that we could look at the subject of our interaction with the world during last night's Meeting of the Minds philosophy meeting. You might think this sounds vague, but I propose it's *very* specific. <u>How we interact with the world</u>. *What else* do we do?

At eight o'clock, we drove to the abandoned northeastern tunnel entrance in front of the Ogden warehouse on the paved way after you turn left at the light before reaching OVMC (if you're coming from the library). We got a flashlight and walked to the tunnel from the parked car. The flashlight died a hundred feet in, so I went back and got another one from the car. This flashlight served us well for the remainder of our "there and back" tunnel walk.

At this point, I'll confess that I'm using the "Royal" 'we.' I was the only one who showed up for this tunnel adventure!

After leaving Keith, I reconnoitered north Wheeling two hours before the meeting, and found, nestled in an overgrown corridor, the other end of this abandoned tunnel directly across from the Wheeling Lowe's—if you take the street in front of the center of Lowe's straight up the hill for four blocks, you'll find yourself there.

To get to the point: "we" walked the whole tunnel, there and back again. It was late, just dark when I finished, and admittedly, somewhat scary. Darkness, the damp, drips of water, echoes. Definitely worth it. A neat experience.

I challenge each of you who are physically up to it to go to this tunnel and to walk it alone. We're doing it anyhow. This seems to be a metaphor.

For me, it was like walking through a sensory deprivation tank with the crunching of gravel being the only sound. I turned the flashlight off as I walked. I would flick the light on again to make sure I was still in the center of the tunnel, and then turn it off. I used the light in the wet places, where dripping water had created a number of shallow ponds in the gravel. Believe it or not, most of the tunnel is dry gravel. There were no snakes, animals or homeless people that I noticed. Around the midpoint, and also, as you near the Lowe's end, it gets a bit wet; you have to step carefully. But there's enough gravel so that you won't get your feet muddy. In places, it feels like being Jesus walking on the water because the gravel is just under the reflective surface, and it seems like you're walking on the surface of the water.

The following is a description I emailed to a friend:

There's a tunnel (the Wheeling Terminal Railroad Tunnel) that I walked through last night. A former train tunnel under a large hill on the northeastern edge of Wheeling. It's a quarter mile long—1,300 feet. I organize a small philosophy group in Wheeling, and I told the guys last week that I wanted us to go through the tunnel for this Tuesday's meeting.

It felt similar to the time I was in a sensory deprivation tank, years ago, in

Pittsburgh at a bookstore called the Eye of Horus on the South Side. I walked on the large-cut gravel covering the tunnel floor. I walked with my flashlight off as much as possible. For my whole transit of the tunnel, I'd see the dusk-lighted end, and it never seemed to grow any closer as I walked toward it. After a couple of hundred yards from the entrance, everything was almost silent and felt muted. The crunching of the gravel under my feet did not echo anymore. I clapped my hands, and this didn't seem to echo much, either. The outside sounds of traffic and city noises were gone. Muffled. Drops of water onto the gravel and into the standing pools of water on the edges of the tunnel were all that I could faintly hear. It felt confined, very still and enclosed. Like a womb to an unborn infant, perhaps. When I turned on the light, I was in a large, silent and expansive-looking place. Like a cave. Turn off the lights, and everything closed in.

On the outside, after emerging, I could see written on the tunnel's keystone, "1890." This was at 8:30. By the time I walked back through the tunnel to where I started, it was completely dark outside. This tunnel walk was like walking through nothingness, with my feet crunching a gravel metronome.

The other guys missed out! Maybe I'll challenge them to go there by themselves and walk through it. I hope they do.

*

Tim, another fellow M&M-er, is being operated on tomorrow morning at 7:30 for a blockage between his pancreas and liver [which turns out to have been pancreatic cancer. Tim is home once again, after spending almost two months in the same hospital where I visited Keith. Most of Tim's time there was spent in ICU, walking through his *own* tunnel].

When I told Tim about my idea to go through the abandoned tunnel as a group, which a local independent film maker had told us about when we were telling stories one night, Tim answered succinctly, "*Hell* no," to my suggestion that he join us. He wasn't feeling his best at that time.

You know, life is a tunnel.

And:

Some people make fun of near-death-experiences and joke to others who are going to be operated on, "If you wake up and find yourself in a tunnel, do *not* go toward the light!"

I think my whole life is that tunnel, where the end I'm heading toward doesn't seem to move any closer as I walk. Looking back, the way I entered seems closer, but then, it, too, is not very distinct; it doesn't seem to be moving away, either.

I am pulled into this world of light and sound on the day of my birth. I close my eyes permanently on the day of my death. Experientially, we have this individual journey between two openings.

A tunnel is bored through a mountain. There are tunnels under bodies of water. My life is a period of stretches of time where I walk, shining the light of my attention here and there, looking up at the curving ceiling or quickly behind me in response to noises I think I hear. When I run in the dark, the light shakes and bounces off the floor and walls; I ignore these surroundings as I run. I hear my breathing and feel my heart pounding in my ears.

There are times when I stop and stand in the darkness. *What's ahead?* When I wonder this, I look at the far-off half-moon profile of the distant entrance. *Where have I been?* prompts me to look back, where I can see the vague shape of the lighted entrance I came through.

Half-way is a funny place. Looking forward and backward, it seems that I'm perfectly still in the center; neither end is approachable, or real. It feels timeless in the tunnel.

I run toward the entrance I've set out to reach. The flashlight plays crazily on all the surfaces, so I turn it off while still running. I run several paces with the light off and all I can hear is the crunching gravel and my breathing.

In the beginning, the distant tunnel entrance seemed like a worthy goal. The safe feeling on the side I entered was reinforced by outside light filtering into the tunnel from behind me, up to about the first few hundred feet.

As I finish my walk, the end is near; the entrance is distinct, and when I turn and look back, *that* far-off opening appears unreal. The end I'm closest to seems more real. I walk out, slowly, looking at the overhanging vines and trees that are grown over the corridor leading to this tunnel. I turn and see the keystone date and the outside tunnel façade.

The journey through the inside tunnel now feels to have been substance-less and dreamlike.

Chapter 22 — Fancypants

Once upon a time, Fancypants, a meek and yet somehow brave, monster, burrowed deeply under the outer wall of a garage in the back yard of an old man who never went into the sagging dry building anymore.

The old man used this garage to store his yard-working tools: rakes, hoes, wheelbarrow, shovels and a long-unused pickaxe. Stacks of empty plastic paint buckets. Piles of wood. Assorted hardware. Used tires. Other things, saved because they could come in handy one day. All of these things were blanketed under a layer of dust and many layers of spider webs covering other spider webs. Dry and rusted, his tools were disused, unused and forgotten. Years before, they had been well-used, worn through this use, and regularly put to use.

In the back corner of the shed:

a circular cutout in the poured concrete floor where a fifty-five gallon drum of motor oil had sat, obligingly, for each of the 25 productive years that this man had actively used the outbuilding. The circular area was now filled by a packed layer of #4 granite rock aggregate. The old man had arranged for a recycler to take away the partially-full drum of motor oil a decade after he retired.

The garage, left long unopened and undisturbed, silently waited for the approaching monster. A sound of moving gravel was the first indication that Fancypants had found his way in.

Tunneling through the earth was easy. Sliding through the moist earth, curving around rocks, roots and buried debris was pleasurable and effortless. Fancypants moved through the earth like an otter moves through the water.

Smoothly, one limb, then another and a slithering long trunk ending with a thick, blunted tail. The tail's end had fallen off in another world and time. Each padded three-toed footstep on the dust-covered concrete left moist prints with liquid clay outlines. Black claws clicked on the concrete.

Fancypants' sticky tongue touched rusting, dusty work implements as the creature slid past the inside walls of the silent, cluttered garage. A hazed, opaque, cracked window let diffuse light in. The monster's slowly deliberate movements did not disturb the dust. Assorted things hung down from the rafters, blocking the penetration of direct light.

Cardboard boxes were up there. None of it mattered.

What did this twelve-foot-long, impossible, underground monster want in the old man's unused shed?

To begin, we must travel forward one million years.

Not only will this old man's garage cease to exist then, along with all, or nearly all, of its contents—so too, will the rural Ohio village this man lives in cease to be; and the organized state of Ohio; and the United States of America; and this human species as it has known itself to be for ten thousand years and a latter-day, more recent, electronic identity and a global "economy"—all of this will be gone as if these things never were.

Nothing will remain in the far-distant present but a thin, oily, rusty layer sandwiched between other sedimentary rock layers, hundreds of feet beneath the surface in places.

Fancypants is from this time.

Our sun appears each morning in that distant location, too, the same as it did for the dinosaurs and for us. A smaller-looking, different-looking, moon still makes its way across the daytime sky and into the night.

In this future present, the nights are truly dark. The Earth has floated away from, and into, an ocean of stars. Never underestimate the power of a million anything.

In this unimaginable distant place, Fancypants is the first of his kind to Return.

In the garage, simultaneous with his unimaginable future, a sharp-edged drawknife leans in the corner near the side door. Five wooden laths lean there, too, one over the other, and long, ropy cobwebs drape from them like unattended scarves. The rusted, slightly-curved drawknife, thirteen inches between its two wooden dowel handles, rests against the garage wall, beneath the aforementioned neatly-stacked straight-grained oak laths.

The old man had been a land surveyor in his youth—one bead on a string of beads of former occupations. These thin hardwood stakes were remnants from that time. Everything in the garage was a remnant from a period of time in this man's life. The drawknife was from a one-month woodworking project, the shaping of rough-hewn barn oak timber bunk beds for his now-grownup and moved-away sons, who had their own families, and who were living in their own productive years, hundreds of miles away from their father's garage.

The time-traveling monster knew nothing of the old man's sons, nor of a human male's productive working life which results, each time, in something approximating this item-filled unused garage.

Shiny, glossy smooth black skin with bright yellow spots showing slight dust markings where dry-rotted cardboard boxes, long-handled implements and a stack of old plastic buckets had been lightly brushed as Fancypants' head moved side to side and his sinuous body moved slowly toward the drawknife corner.

A long, sticky, pale, tan tongue found the cold, sharpened edge. Probing its round handles like an elephant's trunk, Fancypants wrapped his prehensile tongue around the rusting implement, and then carried the drawknife carefully while retracing his steps, backing deliberately to the hole where he'd entered the silent structure.

The monster laid the implement curved-side-up on the dusty concrete at the edge of the barrel hole. Oval wood dowel handles rested on the cold hard surface.

At this time, Fancypants felt what humans would have called the inevitability of the moment. He had known in his cartilaginous bones where and when he was going, and what he would do when he got there; this was the inevitable part. In his reality, there was neither past nor future, only the sprawling present.

If Fancypants had been capable of recognizing the multifaceted experience that humans call fear, he would have said that *his* fear was a fear of not performing a destined task satisfactorily. But this timeless creature knew nothing of anticipatory fear.

Exhaling warmth through his wide, slitted nostrils, Fancypants placed his glistening torso on the drawknife between his lean and powerful forelimbs. With three quick, sawing, back-and-forth motions, he sliced deeply into his body. Dark orange fluid welled from the opening.

The monster nosed into the gravel layer, pushing back through previously penetrated clay soil. Automatically sensing density and porosity, his long body disappeared smoothly into the passage he had created to enter the garage.

Moving through layered soil was as simple for him as a human diving from a springboard into a pool. The subterranean passage behind him was coated now with a trail of viscous fluid from his wound.

Moments after his stubbed tail disappeared beneath the gravel, a tendril of smoke curled upward from the drawknife. The metal glistened blackly, then glowed dull red, and eventually, bright orange. The curved blade drooped and melted. White smoke from its burning wooden handles clouded the garage and hung window-high. When the melting blade touched the concrete floor, it burned the dusty coating there. The wooden dowels burst into flame, transforming into glowing coals and later, fine ash. Twelve hours after Fancypants left, a scorched, thin line that connected two heaps of ash was all that remained.

When the old man died, his sons returned to empty the garage before selling their father's property. The older son toed the mark on the floor near the barrel hole and wondered what had caused it. He returned to sadly nostalgic musings about his dead parent.

As the drawknife glowed, and as it melted into nothingness, Fancypants was twenty yards away and ten feet below the surface, moving through a former tunnel. He angled downward, following an underground seepage of saturated soil where the water table had sent a tendril toward the surface. Twelve feet under the level of the garage foundation, a clutch of newly born, blind salamanders intermingled in an undulating fabric of amphibious bodies. The much larger, wounded, mature shape from another place maneuvered itself over the writhing mass and slowly settled down.

The undeveloped salamanders convulsed in union before melting into a puddle of newly-recombinant DNA sludge. This chimeric soup was drawn into the monster's open wound—wicking into its flesh like water pulled into a dry sponge. The four-meter-long monster was immediately killed.

Individuation, impressions, sensations and impulses winked out.

Suivant:

A dark oval appears on the lower edge of the bulldozer's grade line as it pushes through the dirt.

It is Saturday evening, and the operator guides his machine forward out of the dip and reaches to turn the switch counter-clockwise that shuts the engine down. This time, he doesn't give a shit about the excavator's engine. *Hardcore Excavating* had promised the developer to clear these lots by the fifth, or pay daily fines. As a result, he'd worked twelve to fourteen hour a day with no breaks for two weeks.

"To hell with it. McCandles can do the rest on Monday."

Even as the man muttered this, he knew he'd probably be back tomorrow himself; but for once, he wanted to get out of here before eight.

The excavator's engine heat shield ticked as the metal cooled. His habit of self-talking didn't sound the same in this quiet. In the cab, talking while working was how he thought. Talking aloud with the engine running was like thinking. He slammed the cab door and climbed down the ladder and the crawler tracks to the scraped clay.

Without eyeing the results of his day's work, he walked across the rutted construction site to his pickup. When he yanked the door open in the approaching dusk, he didn't notice the antique DVD case falling onto the ground. In the early morning darkness, it had moved from its careful position by his side. It was pulled forward by his work vest and dropped onto the floorboard to rest against the closed door as he went off to begin his day's work. It remained there between the seat edge and door panel until the moment he opened the door after work, in the near-dark again.

The man pushed his vehicle door wider open to hold the top edge of the cab and to pull himself in with his calloused right hand on the steering yoke. He threw his lunchbox into the vehicle and shoved off the ground with a heavy work boot, hearing a crack at the same time as he felt a brittle crunching under his foot.

He leaned out, looked down, and instantly realized what had happened.

"God damn it!"

He got out of his truck and bent to pick up the vintage petrochemical plastic movie case, hoping.... He prayed to see an undamaged disc, even though he knew he'd probably destroyed the thing. The broken case was bad enough, almost as bad as a damaged disc.

"Shit, shit, shit!"

He repeated this word, mantra-like. The formerly pristine age-brittled disc was now in three distinct pieces; his heel had smashed through the fragile cover and destroyed a prized, long-sought-after 50-year-old video recording.

"Goddamn it, goddamn it...."

The slightly overweight equipment operator shook his large balding head. "Son of a... goddamn...." His swearing was beginning to lose steam.

He went to the front of his truck to examine the disc and case in the LED headlights. Maybe....

After a handful of glum, silent, head-shaking minutes, he dropped the pieces on the hood and looked out over the darkening ground he had pushed for eleven hours.

"Son of a bitch."

He closed the broken pieces inside of their case carefully and Frisbeed the old-fashioned "movie" container in the direction of his excavator, intending to hit the machine.

The spinning rectangular disc case angled off to the left and landed in the clay behind his dozer. It remained closed, resting in a black-smudged, scraped-over oval hole in the smooth clay surface that had appeared after the machine's last push. The oblong hole was filled with an inky-black tar-like substance. The disc case settled face down, sinking into the liquid.

Forty-seven years later, the newly-constructed industrial park was demolished, and another roadway was built in its place, running through the very spot the bulldozer had stopped that day.

Five hundred years later, the country changed names.

Five thousand years later, a volcanic rift split through the place.

Fifty thousand years after that, a marshland extended for hundreds of kilometers; the entire former state was now one continuous swamp. The climate had changed drastically.

Five hundred thousand years after the man broke his recorded disc, a symbiotic civilization raised its collective head from this now-wet portion of the rocky planet.

Half a million years after its humble beginning in the clay of a construction site, what humans clumsily labeled "evolution" resulted in the unlikely dual-race of Symbiotes-Empaths.

"Civilization" wasn't an accurate word; no words were.

Species/being/knowing was closer to what they considered themselves, but interspecies translations are profoundly improbable, especially when there is no language or limiting concept to communicate.

Tens of times "older" than the one it had unknowingly replaced, this class of being used no words; instead, a sophisticated chemically-perfect impression recall faculty completely bypassed the primitive [vocalizing] aspiration-based attempt at information sharing.

Each member consciously knew its genetic identity and "inheritance." Human memory had been a primitive, undeveloped form of this evolved knowing-ability. The salamander-like race called itself nothing, built nothing, and traveled at will through space-time [a primitive, imprecise concept from a long-extinct human species]. The creatures existed on a boundless spectrum. No poets remained, either, to capture their sunsets.

Encoded into their DNA, simultaneously and permanently shared by all species members, a perfectly-preserved carry-over was all that remained of an extinct/existing/previous/current/forever-now-long-gone lifeform:

Fancypants:

Fancypants (2011), comedy/drama, directed by Joshua Russell, starring Patrick Gleason, Roddy Piper, and Robert Carradine. Featuring Nick Turturro, Richard Kind, and introducing Jackson Dunn.

A professional wrestler is afraid of conflict in real life. He is nearing the end of his career and finds out that he has one fan left: an 8-year old boy who hides a secret that will change Leo's life forever. This film was shot entirely on location in Chicago.

"Best Feature" winner at the 2011 Sunscreen Film Festival in St. Petersburg, Florida; the official selection at the 2011 Seattle True Independent Film Festivaland and the

2012 Treasure Coast Film Festival in Fort Pierce, Florida.

Fancypants premiered in Chicago on September 29, 2011. After a limited theatrical release, it was released nationwide on February 10, 2012 via Comcast On Demand, and on March 13, 2012 through Time Warner, Cox, Charter, and all other cable providers. *Fancypants* was distributed in the US by Lightning Entertainment and Entertainment Content Management."

Chapter 23 — Hollow Houses

In empty nests, built-up cumulatively,
Accumulated, repaired, settled into and aged,

Widows sit in chairs
By windows looking nowhere.

I drive past these houses I know are empty,

Where once men lived, too,
Loving and shouting, laughing and aching,

Eventually dying.

As the widows grow older, their husbands' missing presences grow, too.

These widowed old women put Christmas lights around windows and doors,
Halloween pumpkins on porches.
Their cars rest like crypts in silent garages after dusk.
Inside, lit by nightlights, beds in extra rooms are piled high with comforters.

If I didn't know any of this,
I would drive by and think,
"Now *there's* a household,"
As the lights behind curtains and the mowed lawn pass by and grow small behind me.

But, I *do* know.
Like a tree that looks solid until the wind blows, breaking itself in half,
Showing everyone it was hollow.

Chapter 24 — Naturally

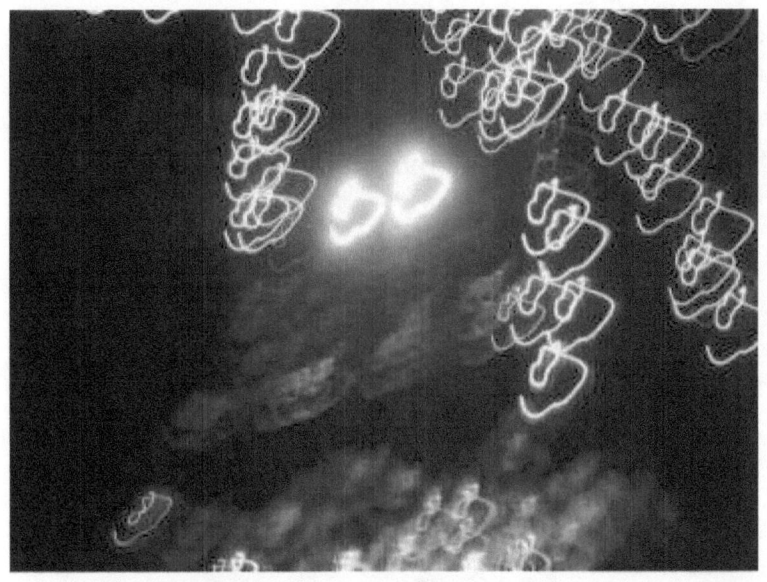

[vingt-trois septembre deux mille treize]

What is the nature of the problem?

It's in his nature.
Nature versus nurture.
To err is human.

What are we, *really*?

"To grasp the immensity of our unknowing," as a friend likes to phrase it, seems a near impossibility.

We get glimpses of the depth of this ignorance that we swim within. I do, at least.

I consider our seeming apparent separation from the animal kingdom. We're animals, I'm told, but why is there such a big difference between other animals and us? Aren't *we* the aliens? Why aren't we just a *little* better off than all the rest? Why is there such a big gap?

Homing pigeons, raccoons, grizzly bears, salmon, ants and the unseen world of bacteria and viruses, not to mention slime molds and blue-green algae—all survive and duplicate themselves without going to school or learning how to drive. Or... do they? Maybe they do all of these things. Everything's relative.

Female turtles bury their eggs—those copied selves—under the sand. When the little ones hatch, they "learn on the job" or die. They guess right or perish. The vast majority dies to be eaten by ocean predators and plucked from the beach by seagulls. If they didn't die in such bountiful numbers, many other species would be hungrier, and would suffer. Like ocean krill, the baby turtles' sacrificial offerings are depended upon and unquestioningly accepted.

An adolescent deer hit the front of my new car last week. That's the way it happened. It was a Tuesday night and I was driving past the Belmont County minimum/medium security prison on Route 331 north.

Deer who don't learn this particular school lesson end up bloated on the edge of the road. Their carrion is appreciated by all who feed upon the result of a mistimed leap into destiny.

Deer, opossum, raccoons.... Me? Do we all have destinies? It depends on what we mean.

I must continue to guess correctly. As a parent, I feel I am on full-time disaster duty, keeping my young from running into the path of a coal truck or a speeding car.

Members of our species seem to feel that we are beyond or above "base" things like animal instincts. What about fear, anger or love? Do we need instructions to feel these things? Aren't they automatic?

Because they're so innate, so self-apparently true, we call our own instincts "common sense" or "street smarts" or, simply, "obvious." We have no objectivity regarding our own automatic reaction patterns. This is my opinion.

Each "normal" person, each weird, eccentric person, is a walking, living, breathing successful testimony of a progenitor's lineage and an unbroken line of fortunately correct guesses. An angry man, a complainer; a glad-hander, a sly manipulator; a liar, a helpless one and the weak are all here because of one reason—they *survived*. Whether by pure, blind total chance or an accidental correct choice or a considered, deliberate strategy... or none of these things. Most likely, all of the above, in a profoundly unique blending of factors.

An adult sea turtle swims sedately at the end of an eternally long daisy chain of circumstances.

We're all here for a *very* good reason. We're a success story; a sequence of unlikely events and choices.

The deer who *don't* dart into my path at night don't get plastered all over the asphalt or smashed into the front of my car—that night.

An angry man, constantly untrusting and wary. A helpless soul whose very essence engenders an assisting instinct in all others, encouraging them to feel sympathy and to use their *own* resources to support this poor, "helpless" individual.

Everything *is* because it works.

"Fun" or enjoyable—or even their opposites—are irrelevant. "Works" means survive.

"Survival of the fittest."

"Natural Selection."

This second item, "natural selection," is probably more accurate, I suspect, because there are some very seemingly "unfit" people who somehow accomplish an awful lot during their lives—and they also live long enough to reproduce themselves! Steven Hawking, the paralyzed physicist, is an example.

My personal reluctant adaptation to an ever-changing environment comes to mind.

Supposedly, it is one of human kind's greatest traits—the ability to adapt to virtually any environment. It's also one of human kind's admittedly least favorite activities: changing anything habitual.

When something goes wrong, I don't welcome it with open arms as an opportunity to adapt or to change something in my life; I complain. My automobile breaks down, rodents tunnel under my porch, a virus sidelines my plans for a vacation. Initially, I experience a strongly negative emotional reaction. Eventually, grudgingly, reluctantly, I accept and adapt to the new, changed, circumstances.

We have natural-to-us characteristics we were born with: long legs, quick reflexes, clever minds, sharp eyes, a competent sense of balance or a keen sense of smell. Each of us has something we are particularly "good" at, that thing which comes "naturally" to us. Some of us exercise and develop this ability to its fullest extent possible; others obviously don't.

This range is referred to as our *potential*. This is my personal observation. You, of course, develop your *own* summarizing explanations to yourself in the course of your own span of time we refer to as "living." What would the sea turtles call its life?

The biggest pity on Earth, I feel, is when a long-legged person doesn't get (or doesn't give themselves) the opportunity to stretch their appendages and strain or run as fast, or leap as far, as they possibly can; or when a strong person doesn't attempt to lift the heaviest load they're capable of lifting; or when a smart person doesn't apply themselves to the greatest, most complicated unsolved problem they can recognize.

My "natural" aptitude comprises my own unique golden highway toward a personal life well- and wonderfully-lived.

What *am* I?

I think that a person could spend a lifetime of observation and thinking about what they really are.

This is as rich and multi-dimensional a subject as our own billions-of-years-long unbroken living-cells-chain of heritage we're accustomed to calling "myself." We living, fleshy fossils.

I do not advocate that every person ponder the deeper meaning of their life—any more than I think everyone should pick up the heaviest load possible, or jump as high as possible. We *should* do what our capacities imply we should do. We should do what we're drawn toward, if you want to put it that way. Again, my opinion. What *else* should we do?

My belief is that each of us should spend our life in exclusive service to our personal inclination potential. Communists paid homage to this notion. Casting a person for their role in a movie. We don't act; we play ourselves, effortlessly.

If someone actually *does* do what they were born to do, then they will become the embodiment of their deepest meaning. Their mature selves. What is their "deepest meaning"? It is that exactly, and not one thing less.

I have lived a number of years unengaged and unsatisfied. I have also lived a number of years engaged in my passion to its fullest, exclusively focusing on my most meaningful interest. One of these periods was colored by regret and unfulfilment. The other was not.

What *else* are you going to do? I think that once we do what we were meant to do, we're freed to do something else, if we want. Until then, we're just unfulfilled potential, dissatisfied; we're stuck, in other words. MOST people appear to live mildly satisfying, mostly unmeaningful (to themselves) lives. Living like that never appealed to me.

Are *you* going to listen to someone else (me) tell you how you *should* live? I am not, nor is anyone, an authority on you. But I want to help you, if I can.

Do you ever pray to a deity, asking for guidance or for a message telling you what you should do?

Are you going to wait for an event to tell you what you should do? Maybe reading this *is* your sign.

It is more than possible for you to wait a LOT of years if you aren't encouraged by these, or other, words toward action. Unfulfilled years flow like water into oblivion, leaving you emptier than when you started. *Do* what your passion is, and you'll have a legacy of fulfillment to ruminate over in your rocking chair years. What value is there to this? Consider the alternate legacy of felt-emptiness resulting from inaction.

Should you give up attempting to choose the "right" thing? Should you, instead, choose to simply react to events and to not purposely "decide" anything? Sometimes, in retrospect, this may be the best way of going about things. Maybe most people are waiting for Godot. Or simply reacting.

I could be wrong, but I think that many people do nothing. Absolutely nothing. They "plan" to do things like quit a job, leave a relationship or move out of an area, but this isn't the same thing as stepping into one's destiny and doing any of those things.

"Walking forward into our destiny" is walking into a <u>fearful</u> place because we've never been there before. We fear the unknown. It's only natural.

Doing nothing fearful is the hands-down, all-time favorite default activity of everyone I have ever known. I see this tendency in myself and in my fellow animals.

I whine, get angry or depressed, abandon difficult-seeming work or avoid beginning it. I grab for the easy return on my absolute minimal investment of time, energy and attention. I escape into diversion. I do little else.

When my toothache dominates my sensory attention and is no longer "ignorable," I pick up the phone and call my dentist, demanding the earliest appointment and complaining when this date is more than a day away.

Is laziness evolutionarily-advantageous?

It *has* to be. It is one of our strongest instincts.

What about hardworking-ness or honesty? Aren't these specific-to-our-species "qualities" (as if they weren't instincts) evolutionarily-advantageous? They can't not be.

My natural tendency is to ponder these kinds of things. This is the weight I bend my own back to. I don't make it into a science; I'm too lazy. But, I have a lot of opinions and a compulsive urge to strive toward an overall comprehension and understanding. Why? You know why. Is my compulsion to understand things evolutionarily-advantageous? Of course; I am.

What *am* I? An apparently thinking animal? What is "thinking"? What about achieving an understanding of my essence, my nature, in its totality? Is there an advantage to *that*? Can a stalk of corn or a turtle become enlightened to the truth of its existence?

With all my soul, I believe it can.

I've seen with myself and others that fortuitous, "good," helpful things come to those who strive in the manner in which they were seemingly made to work. When deep thinkers wholeheartedly think, and high jumpers jump and hard workers work; each becomes something quite different from the hesitator, the do nothing-er. They become themselves.

I'm not advocating a caste system in which people are pigeon-holed into rigid categories. But, maybe I am. Acknowledging that we are all born certain ways might seem judgmental.

I am an admirer of any system which acknowledges innate aptitudes and ostensibly attempts to align individuals with the activities that are aligned with their own capacities.

In my own personal book of truth, a devoted ditch-digger is more than equal to a money-devoted banker, a prestige-addicted politician, a laser-focused ambitious lawyer or an upwardly-mobile medical doctor.

"Stop breathing my air," one fish bubbles to another in this aquarium. *Thus spake the hermit.*

A "loner" is a member of a community of one because he or she has set themselves apart in reaction to how others offend them and their sensibilities.

Whether we want it to be or not, we are members of a self-copying biological identity collectively known as "human."

What *is* a human to a medium-sized crater on the opposite side of our planet's moon, or to the sun our planet is orbiting, or, to a slime mold?

We care about *ourselves* a great deal—as does the slime mold, in its own way.

We are largely defined by our self-obsessiveness. Even while engaged fully in "serving others," which is an ultimate form of obsession with the self. Am I using the royal "we" again? Yes. Always. I do mean "me." Do I care for, or personally interact with the soil, the flora and the fauna in the wooded land that I drive by in my car? I don't care about <u>anything</u>—even when I bulldoze a trail or just walk through these woods.

When I'm digging a ditch, smelling the musk of the earth, I'm distracted for a moment from my perpetual focus on my body and thoughts; I simply transfer my sense of self to an activity. I lose myself by becoming what I'm doing.

<u>I am</u>, as far as I'm concerned, which is odd because I'm almost always, always, always looking out, never in, never looking *here* where I'm looking out *from*.

I recently left my car—not the new one that got hit by a deer, but another—at Foster's Auto, our mechanic repair shop, and I walked seven miles into St. Clairsville to my wife's painting studio. For a solitary character such as myself, a few miles of walking led me to suspect with surprise how far I'd wandered from everything important.

The newest movie, the latest social problem, the next model car, the most recent atrocity visited upon one group by another—a kind of self-flagellation of co-inhabitants of the same species who think they're different from one another. All of this goes on and on and on and on and on.

My fixation on objects within my attention field never ceases. I'm the cat watching a moving red dot. All of my life is a red dot. The snails and I are pattern-following, self-referencing, self-duplicating biological machines.

What is the sound of one reflection-less pane of glass facing itself?

Aggressive yellow jackets each fall; my devoted dog and an adolescent deer who ruined the front of my newest car—we're all interested in being who we are.

In the millions of years that each of its species existed, did any dinosaur stare at the nighttime or daytime moon and compare itself to another species, realizing, with surprise, that it, and every other creature, was the same, in essence—before eating the other creature or being eaten by them?

Did this dinosaur ponder the ultimate meaning of life like I do? Did it wonder about its existence?

What will it take for you to do more than skim over the surface of your self-ignorance?

Did the last dinosaur look at the moon and down at the ground and wonder what it was *all* about? How could it know that it was the last of its kind? We are *all* the last of our kind.

The watering eyes of a bipedal dinosaur and the space-suited feet of a bipedal human have recently touched the same surface.

Chapter 25 — Sunlight

[vingt-sept septembre deux mille treize]

When a red wagon sits on the front yard grass in one place, or a metal Tonka truck or a sun-faded football does, whether for a few days or until the next time I have to mow which is each week, I find light yellow patches shaped precisely like the bottom surface of the object that was resting on the ground. I go through this each week in the summer, and I kick or pull these things to the concrete sidewalk on my first push-mowing pass. In a day, the yellow has faded, replaced by green again.

After leaving a four-foot by eight-foot sheet of half-inch plywood (which I never do) lying on the grass for a week, when I lift it up to look, I find spiders, crickets, millipedes, worms and a very pale yellow-white mat of very, very different-looking grass than that which I'd dropped the board onto the week before.

In two weeks, the grass is pure white, dying, and simultaneously sending long, pale tendrils in search of light. In a month, the grass is disintegrated and mushrooms and fungi have taken over, growing all over the now-exposed surface dirt. Moles have burrowed under the convenient world roof, and ants, millipedes, earthworms and crickets have settled there, too. Growing up on a farm, a board like this would sometimes fall over from leaning against a barn or a fence, and, unnoticed, these things would be happening in the course of a few summer months. I'm sure that a board dropped on any lawn, anywhere, would produce similar results.

I have a hard time imagining an asteroid hitting our planet.

Obviously, I *can* imagine it causing the kinds of devastation that our scientists say took place 66 million years ago. In fact, it's *imaginably* easy to hear the words, "a planet blew up," and experience the mental vision of a round ball exploding into space like that final scene from *Star Wars*. Effortless.

Utter any combination of words, and I'll have a mental image of some kind. What I have a nearly impossible time doing, however, is grasping the magnitude of *any* event, no matter how insignificant or large. The actual impact of such an event, in every sense of the word; this is what I have trouble imagining.

In the waters beneath the northern edge of the Yucatán Peninsula in Mexico, not far from present-day Chicxulub, a one-hundred-and-ten-mile-wide prehistoric impact crater from an asteroid strike hides, unseen. The six-mile-wide *bolide* fireball that plowed into the surface of our planet at this place—it struck the ocean there, actually—was traveling an unimaginably fast 12 miles per second (43,200 miles an hour), and it delivered the estimated energy equivalent of 100 teratons (one hundred trillion tons) of TNT to this bull's-eye on the Earth. This amount of energy was 800 times the human race's world energy consumption for the entire year of 2008. That's a lot of air conditioners and hairdryers left running. The 110-mile-wide crater was also calculated to be 4,414 feet deep.

A thin debris layer covers the Earth from this time, chock full of iridium and "shocked quartz" and can be reliably dated to approximately 66 million years before today. Formerly known as the K-T Boundary, it is now called the K-Pg (Cretaceous–Paleogene) boundary. A blanketing worldwide layer of compressed ash remains from this time. It is surmised that dust and particles covered the entire surface of the earth for as long as ten years after the impact.

Certainly, sunlight was blocked from the surface of the earth by dust particles in the atmosphere. Naturally, this long-term shadow would have cooled the surface dramatically—or so I imagine; I know that I get cold sitting in the shade. Sun-dependant plants' photosynthesis would have halted. This fact alone greatly affected the entire food chain of the planet, as countless creatures depended on eating plants, and these plants, sadly, would have been dead.

Everything I have just said is an abominable understatement.

Just as saying, "A dog died," is an incredible understatement to that dog. What the dog experiences is much more to the dog than our three words can convey.

We, apparently, know that an asteroid at least ten kilometers across (six miles) slammed into the earth just off the coast of Mexico 66 million years ago, releasing two million times more energy than the most powerful thermonuclear bomb ever exploded. This is *another* understatement.

Millions of tons of rock (another pitiful understatement), with trees, grass, dinosaur parts and insects, were ejected out of Earth's atmosphere into space—into space. *Really?* Yes. Falling back to the Earth on ballistic trajectories and reheated by atmospheric re-entry, this debris is believed to have superheated the air across the entire planet, igniting the world's forests. All of them. Yes. Again, yes. Can this be possible? *Is* it possible to imagine such an understatement? *Thus thought the ant....*

Shockwaves radiating outward faster than the speed of sound (faster than 761 miles an hour at sea level) triggered earthquakes and volcanoes. *Mega tsunamis*, thousands of meters high (a meter is the same as a yard), spread outward from the Chicxulub impact area, pounding coastlines and traveling hundreds of miles inland on every landmass around the world.

And so. Dust filled the sky and rained back down onto the earth as mud. The darkened atmosphere prevented photosynthesis and plants on land and in the water could not produce energy and survive. The entire food chain, as it had formerly been, disintegrated. A pitiful understatement.

This planet—our planet—grew colder. Dust and various microscopic particles remained suspended in the atmosphere for decades. *Years* of acid rain, and eventually global warming, resulted as the massive quantity of carbon from incinerated, blasted and dissolved life filled the Earth's atmosphere. This layer in the atmosphere trapped the longer wavelengths, the infrared spectrum of electromagnetic radiation resulting from captured shorter wavelength radiation—what we call "sunlight"—and these "trapped" radiated thermal wavelengths remained closer to the planet's surface. This is the "greenhouse effect."

Picture yourself in a closed car in a parking lot on a sunny day. The outside temperature doesn't matter as much as the fact that the window glass lets in sunlight but doesn't allow the interior thermal radiation to get back out. The inside of the car you're sitting in heats up. Things are heated by the sunlight, and these "heated" things radiate "warmth."

All of the above effects, affecting all planetary life, were devastating, and this is the most profound understatement of the largest, saddest, kind.

I try to imagine what it was like, but I can't imagine even one of those days, let alone a stretch of endless weeks, months, years, decades, hundreds of years, thousands of years, millions of hours upon hours of ceaseless change—before such things as human beings and their concept of "years" came into being. All of this change occurred because a single, six-mile-wide, rock hit this 7,918-mile-wide planet we consider home.

I can't imagine my four-foot by eight-foot sheet of plywood covering my whole yard, my whole village, my whole northeastern county in Ohio, my whole life—my children, my wife, my pets and me—and remaining for years... for decades. It amazes me that mushrooms aren't the only dominant species on this planet, writing essays and building buildings these days. Maybe they are. Maybe that's where bacteria and viruses really got their leg up.

Sixty-six million years ago is an uncomprehendable number. "Ago" is an elusive, fuzzy concept. Six hours? Six minutes? A lifetime ago? What does this "ago" feel like? Imagine *anything*. Do it *now*, before a minute passes, and you'll be bored, and your attention will be wandering, aimlessly.

What were the last, pre-cataclysm days of dinosaurs like before this disaster? What about the last days of the dinosaurs immediately following the impact? The latter span of days was very likely not pleasant—not even for carnivores or carrion eaters. Obviously, my small, nose-twitching ancestors were competent carrion eaters; otherwise they would not have survived to pass their baton on to me and to my children. That final loooooong all-you-can-eat dinosaur buffet must have been really something (another understatement).

All I can think to say is: *Thank you, God—thanks, killer-of-all-dinosaurs asteroid—for my children's lives.*

This asteroid was ten kilometers across—six miles—and it's about fifteen miles to the Wal-Mart in St. Clairsville where I buy hotdogs, windshield washer and cat litter. It takes me twenty minutes to pull into the parking lot after backing out of my own driveway. What a *small* thing that asteroid 66 million years ago was! What a huge, small thing. Planetary scientists say that it killed 75 percent of all animal and plant species on Earth.

Impacts on this scale have happened uncountable times before; our planet—all planets, in fact—was created through accretion, and impacts such as this will happen countless times again in the lifespan of our planet. "Countless" for more than one reason; we will likely not be around to count these events. An uncomfortable thought, to say the least. Did the dinosaurs ever ponder this possibility?

Our planet was created by things slamming into it with unimaginable violence (unimaginable to we, to us, to ants). *All* planets were created equal in this violence. There was no God's magic wand. Or, maybe it was a conductor's baton keeping time to the impacts.

Our currently-accepted model of solar system formation is the popular acceptance of what our contemporary scientists theorize about the formation of orbital bodies in the observable universe. Stars are created like this. Today we see the first lights of new stars glowing inside intergalactic nebulae—the ghosts of former stars.

An "accretion disc" forms around a proto-sun, which is composed of gravity-compressed gasses and interstellar dust. Self-attraction, that magical thing "gravity," does all the heavy lifting. Our Hubble space telescope has stunningly wonderful images of stars in every phase of their life cycle, from creative birth to explosive death.

Millions of years; hundreds of minutes; sixty seconds, and even now, during this pleasantly sunny Monday afternoon.

Intervals of time are utterly arbitrary and wholly dependant on our brains, which concoct them and then consider these self-made lengths of duration with awe and amazement or indifference; without us, our time intervals don't exist. How much time is there between blinks—to an eyeless rock?

Yet, the sun *does* exist. Sunlight, too. Rocks and us, as well. What does "exist" mean? Do you have to be aware to exist?

Today began cool and sunny. There were no clouds overhead as my wife and I walked with Mike, our English Labrador, around an oval, hillside gravel path in our village park.

Days are noticeably longer in the summer heat and much shorter during the colder winter. Leaving something on the lawn in the well-lit summer kills the grass quicker than I would have imagined. I tell my sons to pick up their toys and balls when I see they've left them on the grass. I get badly sunburned without sunscreen in the summer, especially on the sand or near the water at the beach, or, in a pool; I get baked pretty good by all the ultraviolet reflection. In the fall or winter, when it's cold, I am able to enjoy the sun's warmth because it doesn't burn me very much.

As pleasant as the sun feels on my face today, this moment, the Earth and my home and family and lawn would be a frozen-solid block, if not for the atmosphere holding in a portion of the constant stream of radiation pouring out of our local star. We have an atmosphere, with wind and rain and ocean waves and storms.

Our days are numbered. I'm sorry. I ignore this, too, as much as I can. I know it's true, from a cosmic point of view.

When I can, though, after mowing, I close my eyes, lean back in my folding beach chair and soak up the sun.

Chapter 26 — Disintegration

The disintegration of me
is easy to see.

Me....

The sand beneath my feet

wears my feet

Smooth, wears the shells and rocks, wears everything

of everything,

and me, too,

watching.

I am a shell under the feet of the sea.

My defeat whispers

softly. My feet

push into the sand and heel into the coolness below,

into everything.

Disintegration is easy.

I stand sideways and waves push and pull, crash and recede,

smoothing,

polishing,

wearing me.

Free.

Chapter 27 — Life

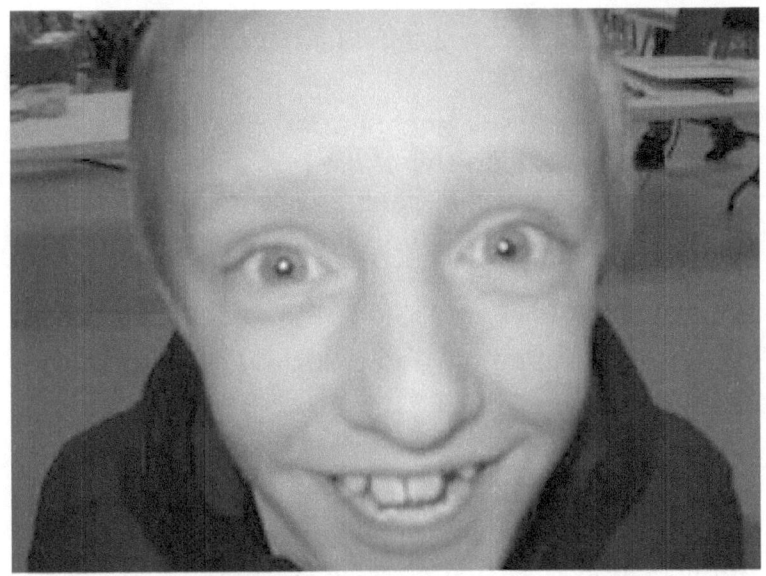

Curious and creative.

Clinging and irreverent.

Self-appreciative in proportion to proximity to threatened oblivion.

Self-replicating.

Self-referencing.

Self.

Concepts of Self radiate outward from a center of self.

Concepts of Self transform into concepts of Ultimate Beings responsible for observable phenomena.

No constructs of "separate" individuation exist with the absence of life. "Self" is not nothing. "Existence" is separation, manifestation, arising from the field-of-all-possible-things.

Every concept is an explanation to the self by the self about the self.

Life *must* explain all encountered phenomena. This is the font of religion. All of life possesses the ability to sense an external-to-itself environment with which it interacts. What does "sense" mean to the environment? There is an interwoven web of life sensing life sensing environment.

Information is imperative to a solitary prime directive: *Survive*.

What is the first explanation story that every immature, developing member of a (collection of identical individuals) species tells itself?

What? *Oh*. Only the human species has language, you say. *Ho-ho*. And the *other* animals don't have to make sense of their world? Don't they have to know what's going on? Don't they have to survive? Amoebas appear to interact with their environment.

What is the first explanation story that *you* made up for yourself? That your parents were right? Your family's view of the world *was* the world?

What is curiosity? Apart from how it *feels*?

What is creativity, apart from how it *feels* during an act of creation? What does it feel like to build a sand castle?

What is "clinging," in, and of, itself? Does it mean to hold onto something emotionally? What does emotional mean?

What is a "lack of appreciation"? What *isn't* important to an individual crawling across a Petri dish?

Is an "increase of appreciation" even possible?

What does threatened "self-extinction" mean to a self-involved, self-contained, self-organized entity— meaning you, me, a virus, an earthworm and the ancient alien lifeform? Isn't the ability to replicate oneself immortality? Isn't it, at the very least, magical?

If immortality is living forever, we're all immortal... so far.

Doesn't count, you say. Does immortality need a continuously-existent individual consciousness? Does it need *you*? Is the universe conscious? Immortality wouldn't exist without you, you argue, because without you there's no one to remember that you're immortal.

Is there another form of consciousness or memory that you're not aware of?

Is DNA memory?

Isn't a newborn the literal embodiment of a <u>species memory</u>? A living, breathing, 3-D copy. Isn't this undeveloped creature a faithful copy, a "memory" of the species?

Do *you* have to feel every sensation that your child feels in order for you to consider that child valid? "Of course not," you say.

Does your great-great-grandfather need to inhabit your every thought in order for you to exist? He does, you know. Isn't he immortal, then, through you?

Where is the passing of the baton of consciousness? Consciousness simply "appears" inside of us at a certain point? Is that it? A certain critical mass of neurons? It appears, coincident with a critical mass of cells within a life form as this life form grows more developed. Is that it? Is there consciousness in the tree?

Every self is conscious. Every single self. What is a "self"? We believe in our individual experience that we are separate and unconnected to those before us, or, to those who will remain alive after us. We are "us." We habitually say, "I."

There is something more going on, because we've "inherited" certain characteristics, certain traits or certain design features or flaws from our grandparents and from those a thousand or a million years before *their* grandparents. Don't you realize that you think with those other individuals' thoughts? How could you not?

You just appeared? Woops, here comes God. Were you, or where you not, born of your mother? Really, what *does* life mean? When did life first appear in the universe? Where, and why?

Do I need immortality? I surely think I do. I need my children. Does the dandelion seed "need" immortality like I do?

Show me a person who "decides" not to reproduce and I'll show you the end of an immortal, timeless conglomerate stretching back to the beginning of cell mitosis on this planet from their present cappuccino-drinking empty-feeling or contented-feeling selves.

What else can a self do other than explain everything it encounters to itself in terms of itself? What else can *I*, this amoeba, do? Are you any different?

Life results from its roots anchored in the rich soil of death. Every characteristic stems from a perpetual balancing act, performed without nets, over oblivion.

What *is* death? The cessation of collective cellular activity? Can a rock exist without my observation? Can existence still "be," without me?

If life is eternally dropping shells of itself as it grows and continues forward, year after year... what *is* life, <u>really</u>?

Chapter 28 — A Day in the Life

Yeah.

We were sitting on the porch swing in the near-dark morning. Andrée signaled to the bus with two hands; she had thought the bus driver was going to pass by.

Bus stops, folding door opens, Ben and Gui climb on, door shuts, slight pause, bus accelerates. We wave at the darkened-windows school bus. Andrée says, "Cold," hugs herself and goes inside. Mike, our Polar-bear-white English Labrador, quickly stands from lying on the wooden porch floor to follow *Mommy*. He knows who this word means very well. I get up and go inside, too. The porch swing moves alone behind me.

Monday morning, and much colder today than yesterday. Yesterday was very warm—okay, it was hot—and very humid and sunny. Above all, it was sunny. A great day for air conditioners. This morning is cool—cold, even—although once again sunny, even though it rained all night until just before seven this morning when the boys were getting on the bus.

Yesterday was quite a day.

Memories of the sun and heat, with our feet in the running cool water of the various pools in a water feature constructed of stone blocks that step down a gradually-sloped hillside between the Pittsburgh Pirates baseball stadium and the Pittsburgh Steelers football stadium on the North Shore of the headwaters of the Ohio River. This water feature is across the river from Point State Park, which is a peninsula between the Monongahela and Allegheny Rivers. The Ohio River begins where these two rivers meet.

Our two young brothers took off their shirts and sat in the step-down waterfalls. They splashed in the shallow pools on different levels of the water feature. We hadn't planned on sleeping. For the most part, Andrée and I sat on two massive square-cut stones off to the side, in the shade, occasionally taking photos of the boys with her iPhone since we didn't have our digital camera with us. In shorts, I walked barefoot, down and back up again over the multi-level black stone waterfall. The water rose to my knees when I moved through the pools, making my way past other splashing kids with their parents. I sat down again near Andrée on a not-too-wet square of stone in the shade of some overhead tree branches.

Later in the afternoon:

We were at a small playground on the edge of Panther Hollow in Schenley Park. This area borders Oakland, which is home to the University of Pittsburgh, where I'd graduated nineteen years earlier.

In the playground, I encouraged my older son, Guillaume, to hang down from a piece of playground equipment and drop to the ground. His younger brother had been eager to show us that *he* could do it, but I told him to wait until Gui had gone first. Ben's own first time dropping was fearful; I could see it in his eyes—but he had wanted to show us that *he* could do it better than his older brother.

Fifteen minutes later, we are throwing Gui's Nerf football in the open grass area of the park. Two kids, also pre-teen brothers, approached our boys to ask if they could play football, too. Andrée and I gave them permission and we walked around the park while the boys played.

Four boys—two sets of brothers; two black brothers and two white—played touch football in the open lawn shade of large trees that line the asphalt drive bordering the park to a cul-de-sac turn-around. Andrée and I walked to the end and back, talking.

Before this snapshot in time, earlier in the day for lunch, we had eaten at *Big Jim's* under a tall bridge. A friend of mine named Jim turned 82, and several of us were there to give him gifts, eat cake, and sing "Happy Birthday." We talked in pairs and in groups. It felt like a family reunion, and it was, in a way. We were related to our mutual fondness for Jim. All of us had been to Jim's 80th birthday party in this same dark restaurant—an old stomping ground from Jim's self-described "drinking days" of four decades past. Andrée, the boys and I missed last year's 81st bash.

For this 82nd birthday gathering, Gui had brought a cardboard box filled with a variety of *Sarris* chocolate bars and chocolate-covered pretzels. He was fundraising for a school trip his class was taking to Washington D.C. the following year [they've already taken it]. Next year, he will be in the eighth grade [he is, now].

I was proudly watching him approach strangers; he must really want to go to D.C., I realized, because approaching strangers and initiating a conversation with adults isn't something most kids enjoy or excel at. Somewhere between eating lunch and leaving, I pulled up a chair and sat next to Jim. I asked him what the best thing about being 82 was. He said, "Ask me next year around this time and I'll let you know."

Earlier, again, the first thing we did when we got to Pittsburgh was drive up to Mount Washington, a ridgeline community overlooking the Monongahela River, 447 feet above its southern bank, directly across from the downtown Pittsburgh skyscrapers. Immigrant steel mill workers used to live here. Before that, coal miners. From the height of the road and sidewalk along the top of Mount Washington, you can see Point State Park's fountain at the tip of the downtown triangle. Below, the "Mon" and Allegheny rivers hand their batons to the Ohio River, which forms there.

From Mount Washington, easily more than a dozen bridges spanning three rivers are viewable. On *this* glorious sunny day, the view was breathtaking. For me, it *always* feels uplifting when I come here, no matter what the weather. That's why I make a point of coming here first. We left our car parked on Grandview and walked down to the top of the incline.

We rode the Monongahela Incline (to my boys' amusement, Andrée always refers to it using the Latin-derived word, "funicular"), one of two surviving incline cable railways on tracks in this area, down the steep slope to Station Square on the east bank of the Mon. We walked across the Smithfield Bridge, observing floating river traffic below us. An amphibian tourist bus boat was entering the river slowly from the downtown side river bank.

At the Wood Street subway station downtown, we took the underground "T" to Heinz Field, home of Gui's favorite team, the Pittsburgh Steelers. The trolley system downtown runs underground and then above ground again to cross the river before stopping at an elevated station just outside the football stadium. We walked around the entire stadium and then continued along the river boardwalk to the aforementioned stone block water feature where our boys swam. It was a beautiful day, a stunning "Indian Summer" day. We made our way past the Pittsburgh Pirates' PNC Park baseball stadium where the crowds were gathering because of a playoff game later in the afternoon. The Pirates were on a run in their division. After swimming in the water feature, we found the underground North Side "T" station, caught a trolley back across the Allegheny River, under downtown, back above ground and over the Monongahela River to the converted train station at Station Square. From there, we walked to the Monongahela Incline and caught an upward traveling car ten seconds before it ascended to Mount Washington where our car was.

We were able to talk our way into a vacating third floor apartment on Grandview Avenue. Looking out the window, fifty feet higher than the scenic overlook platforms that jut out along Grandview, we were treated to an even more astounding grand view than the one along the road. Having walked and run around for enough hours to earn our hearty midday meal, we drove to Big Jim's in lower Greenfield to eat lunch before Jim's birthday party began.

A few hours later, at the end of Jim's gathering, our assembled reunion crowd slowly broke up and Jim caught his chauffeured ride—Keith pushing Jim's wheelchair—to the front door. We said our goodbyes and drove off in our rental car. Our just-bought-brand-new-car was being repaired after getting hit by a deer. After Jim's, we drove to the University of Pittsburgh Oakland campus.

Across from the Carnegie Library, a maybe-drunk black man was sitting on a black polished granite ledge around a small dried up fountain, body stiff as a board. He might have been drunk; or crazy. He might have been on drugs. I suspected he was homeless. His thin frame was stretched out, board-straight, and he slowly balanced, tipping back and forward like a stick on the edge of a glass. Maybe he was having a seizure. I looked carefully. The boys pushed their scooters by, rolling along the wide stone walkway. Andrée and I walked after them and I kept an eye on the board-stiff man. I hoped he wasn't dying.

Inside a sycamore-lined corridor that stands between the Carnegie Museum of Natural History and Oakland Carnegie Public Library and a large open lawn area across from Forbes Avenue, (itself, opposite the 535-foot-tall Cathedral of Learning), two university students had a "slack line" stretched between two stately sycamores. The line was attached about a foot and a half above the ground. A slack line is a wide, flat nylon strap and a ratcheting "come along" that is stretched between two anchor points. It's tight, but... slack. They took turns balancing on it; this was a variation on tightrope walking.

As we approached, the two college students asked Guillaume and Ben whether they wanted to try. Of course! This was our almost family ritual; we'd encountered this same slack line club in the sycamore-lined area on two other occasions. Different trees, though. We always have interesting conversations with the slack line club members.

Gui and Ben walked back and forth several times in their socks, taking turns holding onto my arm and the arm of the younger slack liner. Andrée walked back and forth once, very proudly (she was ordinarily quite afraid of falling). I tried walking unsupported, falling and rolling on the ground a few times. I said I wanted to make five unsupported steps. I managed four. Nine-year-old Ben was able to take six steps by himself before stepping off. Gui, three. We could have stayed there until dark. We could have stayed anywhere we'd been that day so far until dark.

We thanked the slack liners and urged our boys onward, to cross Forbes Avenue to a blocked-off Bigelow Boulevard between the Cathedral of Learning and the orange brick ten-story William Pitt (student) Union building. It was Sunday. Students were helping a crew disassemble a large elevated performance stage, rolling electrical equipment up ramps to a waiting 18-wheeler. It must have been a big weekend event.

Gui now rode the less-desirable "thumper" scooter, whose back wheel had a flat spot resulting from a long skid down the sidewalk by our house. Each boy prolonged his time riding the "good" scooter for as long as possible.

We visited the food court bathrooms in the basement cafeteria level of the union building and sat outside on a sandstone wall that followed a sidewalk on the Forbes Avenue side of the Union. It was humid and hot but the evening was approaching and it felt cooler in the shade of several large trees. Andrée and I watched Ben scooter smoothly down the sloping sidewalk to a bronze sculpted panther. Our younger boy leaned his scooter against the sculpture base and climbed up to sit between the cat's front paws. Ben likes animals—his stuffed animals, our big, white "fuzzy bunny" dog, Mike, and now this large sculpture of a predator cat. Gui hovered nearby on his "thumper" scooter.

As early Sunday evening arrived, I wanted to visit my friend Tim in ICU room 357 at Wheeling Hospital. It was an hour away. The hospital was on our way home. We live twenty-five miles past Wheeling, further west into Ohio and then eight miles from the exit off I-70. Tim had been in ICU for three weeks.

Our Dodge Avenger rental car got to 100-miles-per hour fairly smoothly along one section of southbound I-79.

"Why don't we go this fast in *our* car?" Ben asked.

"These aren't really race cars," I said, letting the car slow down.

A minute earlier, a new Chevy Camaro had passed us like we were crawling and I thought it was *probably* safe, from a not-getting-a-speeding-ticket point of view, to give the boys their first hundred-mile-per-hour ride in a car. Keeping an eye on the rearview mirror, after announcing that we'd reached the milestone, I let the car drop back down to a sedate 70 m.p.h. Hitting one hundred for a second or two also wouldn't hurt in getting us to Wheeling Hospital a little faster. I was a bit worried about being too late for visiting hours.

We had until eight o'clock, but Tim would probably be tired and I didn't want to get there at the last minute.

Leaving the boys in the waiting room, we asked the intercom camera box outside the closed doors of ICU if we could visit Tim. After hearing, "Sorry, no," we retrieved the boys and went to the elevators. Ben pushed the ground floor number 1. As the doors were closing, we were surprised when they lurched back open and a young African-American woman stood there, looking at us. Andrée asked, "Do I know you?" My wife has met thousands of people during her social painting classes at her art studio, and she often meets familiar-looking people she'd previously spent time with at a painting evening.

"I don't know," the woman answered. "What's your name?"

"Andrée," Andrée said, Americanizing her French name by pronouncing the 'r's like we do here.

"And Dave," the woman finished, stepping into the elevator.

My mind wasn't working yet. "How do you know us?" I asked. Then it slowly dawned on me. "You're Tim's daughter—from Pittsburgh!" She nodded, smiling.

"We were just there," I said.

Paige had come out from ICU looking for us to say that we could come in and see her dad for a few minutes.

"We can go back up to three," she said, after the elevator doors opened on the ground floor. We all laughed as Guillaume pressed the number 3.

I told Paige I could see a strong resemblance between her and her dad.

Back upstairs, Gui and Ben stayed in the empty TV room again while Andrée, Paige and I went through the ICU doors.

We told Tim's daughter about walking the North Shore and swimming in the water step feature.

"Did you see the duck?" she asked.

"Yes!" I answered. I was standing at the foot of Tim's bed. "They have a 50-foot-tall rubber duck in the water at Point State Park," I explained to Tim. "It's right near the fountain."

Tim shrugged. *So what?*

It occurred to me that news of a big yellow duck on the water in Pittsburgh wasn't the most pressing thing he'd been confronted with during his time in ICU.

After a handful of minutes saying we were glad to see him, I had my baseball cap back on and we were saying goodbye to Tim and his wife, Marlene.

We thanked them for letting us visit so late in the day. Paige walked with us to the ICU entrance.

"He needs this," she told us.

I wasn't sure how I would feel, being in a hospital room for three weeks, trying to recover from life-saving surgery.

Later, Andrée and I agreed that it might simply feel good to know that people care. It probably felt good to get visitors that you like, too.

I hadn't wanted to tire out my friend discussing unimportant or even important things....

Twenty minutes after leaving the hospital, we pulled into the parking area in front of Andrée's *Fine Art à la Carte* painting studio in St. Clairsville.

We were here because Gui wanted to count the number of candy bars and chocolate-covered pretzels still left. Andrée had these fundraising treats in her studio for her customers to purchase; there were a handful left in the wicker basket on a table in the corner.

At school the next day, Gui was supposed to turn in all the money he'd raised so far. He wanted to make sure the amounts agreed—that the money he'd collected compared favorably to the number of unsold chocolate bars left. I was skeptical.

As a high schooler, I sold boxes of M&Ms to raise money for a band trip to Toronto. Actually, I don't remember fundraising very much. I *do* remember feeling guilty about not doing a good job at it, and I remember eating more than a few boxes of peanut M&Ms. I also remember having to use my own money to pay for the rest of the box I'd originally brought home to sell to other people. I only "sold" one box.

Gui sold more than one box. It warms my heart to see my children doing better than me.

Fifteen miles after leaving the studio, we were home in Flushing, Ohio. Gui and Mom counted and determined that he had one dollar extra. It was a tip from one of Andrée's customers. "If you give me a dollar," Gui told his younger brother, "I'll give you a pretzel." Ever the salesman....

This salesman never had such an easy sale. Ben *loved* the chocolate covered pretzels and bought a pack every day with his allowance money until we told him to stop using all of his hard-earned chore money buying his brother's candy. It was like having a chocolate store at home. So the chance of another package of pretzels for *half* the price must have been irresistible.

I gave the boys their Sunday wages from a previous week's dishes, cat box, trash and pooper-scooping chores. Ben gave Gui a dollar and smilingly accepted another plastic-wrapped, double, chocolate-covered heavenly pretzel pack.

Mike was glad we were home. He'd had visitors, but they're not his own pack. Faith, a good friend and mother of Ben and Gui's friend Charlie, had let our "fuzzy bunny" outside earlier. Our bunny weighs 110 pounds. "Most of it, hair," I tell people. I'm not joking as much as they think. Andrée's friend Beth, who is Ben's fifth grade teacher, came over after that to feed Mike in the early evening when we called from the road as we left Pittsburgh.

Beth's dog, Franklin, a droopy-eyed long-eared Beagle Basset Hound cross, hosts his friend when we're out of town for more than a day. When Beth is gone, Franklin's adopted mother, Andrée, along with Mike and the boys, visit him a few times a day.

Since he already ate, Mike wasn't hopping up and down, barking his ear-splitting deep-throated "I'm hungry!" He was just very glad that his pack was back.

Big Jim's famously large portion size ensured we were well-fed, as well, with a reheated evening meal. Watching an HGTV home-hunting show in our bedroom as the boys alternately showered and brushed their teeth, Andrée and I discussed enjoying the day.

"We should do that every month."

"Yeah," I said, getting up and heading into the hall. "I'm going to get the boys moving."

Ben was brushing his teeth, dripping wet from the shower. On the other side of the shower curtain, Gui was doing his part to add as much steam as possible to the inside air.

"Wrap it up, boys," I said. A subdued duet of "Yes, Dads" ensued.

Ben and Mom said their nightly prayers in Ben's room, with Gui's "Amen" joining from his room at the other end of the hall. After that, the adults went downstairs. Andrée began to fall asleep on the couch as we watched (alternating between commercials), another house-searching episode and a rerun of Stan Lee's *Superhumans*.

"Goodnight," I said as she made her way sleepily upstairs. "I'll be right up."

"Don't fall asleep in front of TV."

"I won't," I answered. By now, we both knew I probably would.

I closed my eyes. Oops. I switched the channel to "Me TV" and watched part of a black-and-white *Twilight Zone* episode.

Turning off the TV and the cable box with two different remotes, I collected Andrée's glass, two small plates and my own empty glass.

"Go to bed," I said, pointing to the corner in the dining room behind the boys' Lego City. Our large polar bear-looking dog padded to his cushion and plopped down with an old man sigh.

I turned off the lights, leaving one of the cats curled up on a blanket in the corner of our L-shape couch. I put the dishes in the sink and walked up our creaking stairs. Brushed teeth and the rest.

Lying in bed in the dark, I set the alarm for six and pulled the covers over me.

The last acts of a day.

My friend in the hospital, and everybody else formerly alive and to-be-alive, experience their days no differently. But mine are mine.

After dreaming and sleeping, I woke just before four and heard raindrops hitting the hood of the bathroom exhaust fan on the roof. I stood in the dark. Hearing rain hitting that lightweight aluminum overhead always makes me feel good. I sleep better and rest better. I padded back through the darkness and returned to bed.

Chapter 29 — And So It Goes

Beautiful.

I was mowing my lawn. The sky was sublime.

I was steering that God-blessed riding mower around and around, through and through the grass. It was cool, sunny and perfect.

Earplugs in, scratched safety sun glasses on, worn and torn flannel zip-up jacket with sleeves too short on my outstretched arms holding onto the steering wheel. I had already push-mowed—the opposite of my usual pattern—because the lawn was heavy with Saturday's rain and near-frozen dew had lingered on from the night.

I had tried a beginning lap with the riding mower around my bowl-shaped, nearly-acre-lawn, like always. I didn't think it would work, but I wanted to try. The mower kept bogging down and I had to shake the deck repeatedly up and down to unplug the wet, clumping grass from its open, clogged maw.

I was on a schedule; I didn't want to wait until later in the day to begin mowing. I had a lot to do, and this slower mowing would make my outside working time longer. I am a slave to my desired-outcome nature.

So, after a first lap with the riding mower I parked it behind the house on the level ground behind our elevated deck. I tied on my soccer cleats and started to push-mow around the house and on all the steep areas. The sun would dry the main lawn by the time I picked up riding mowing where I left off, I thought. I mowed the small front yard patch of grass and all of the side steep hills. Normally, I do it the other way around.

I walked behind the push mower. It felt like a dream. The light was still sublime. I can't say that too much.

An hour and a half later, after slipping on the hillsides, cleats clogged full of wet packed grass and mud, after leaving occasional bare mud streaks behind me on the hills where my feet slipped when straining to hold the mower deck when I pushed forward, the hard work was done and I was back on the riding mower, hoping the sun had dried the grass enough.

At this time, Andrée drove away to attend church down the street. Service begins there at eleven. My older son appeared up by the house near a privacy fence I'd built in an "L" shape where I park my car. He ran down the tiered grass hills to ask if I needed any help—a condition I assumed his mom made for his staying home with his brother. I braked, adjusted the idle lower and disengaged the mower blades.

"I don't want to stop and pick up any toys or sticks," I said, gesturing around our bowl-shaped yard. "Clear the yard of everything."

My younger son ran down the hill by the fire pit, followed by our bounding, white polar bear dog, Mike.

Two concentric rings around the yard later, I saw both boys swinging under our huge four-trunk maple tree with a tree house on the western edge of our property. Slow-seeming ellipses, legs dangling, arms straight out, hands gripping handle bars removed from absent BMX bikes. I'd attached these two sets of handle bars to the end of doubled-up ropes and cables connecting them to the soaring branches high overhead.

Mike sat nearby on the sloping ground, back legs sprawled; Gui and Ben swung over and over him from two rope swings, tracing two offset circles directly over his unperturbed head.

"Priceless," I said, hearing my own voice the way you do when you're wearing earplugs and the riding mower is loud. I meant it. I always do.

"And So It Goes" is me, the author of a stitched-together collection of narratives all focused on some aspect of individuation, addressing *you*, my reader. It's me talking to me, as well.

Writing is a solitary pastime. Unsurprisingly. Thankfully, maybe. Reading is a lone journey, too—even if you're reading these words aloud to an auditorium filled with people; each individual accepts or rejects what they hear.

And So It Goes, Billy Joel's song, was playing in my head over and over when I awoke this mowing morning—just like this riding mower cutting repeated lazy, grass-blowing undulating grooves around my bowl-shaped, sun-dappled, green, early fall backyard.

Joel's song seems to be one of forlorn bitterness, written about and addressed to a lover who has hurt him—or who *will* hurt the singer.

Tonight, after the magical mowing and sublime light of fall, Andrée will go to bed. Commentless, as is her periodic wont. And so it goes.

And I will stay downstairs watching *Sunday Night Football* on the couch. After eleven, I awaken from a slumber and turn off the TV. I turn off the lights and walk upstairs. I brush my teeth, change into PJs and find my bed in the dark.

> *"And every time I've held*
> *a rose*
> *It seems I only felt the*
> *thorns*
> *And so it goes, and so it*
> *goes*
> *And so will you soon I*
> *suppose...."*

I like the wistfulness of the melody. And yet, its lyrics are a bit too... bitter... for me. The song's stanza is poignant and telling—telling what men of sensitivity and women who had expectantly demanded their notion of perfection feel about their experiences with each other—with the one person they've allowed past their usual superficial defenses.

I heard Joel on an interview series, "Inside the Actors Studio," tell James Lipton, its host, that he'd written *And So It Goes* to explain to his daughter why he was breaking up with her mother. Maybe that was another song he was talking about.

In *this* song, I am able to relate effortlessly to Billy Joel's words and melody.

A rose *is* undoubtedly beautiful. Is it beautiful because it is the color of our own blood? Is love only beautiful from a distant time and place?

When I'm inside of a relationship, with the tidal pullings of the moon and billions of years of subtlety at work, I am pricked by the thorns. Not all the time. Not every time; but the thorns do draw blood every time and the wounds take time to heal. *Beautiful*. And this beauty has a price exacted in pain. What is "pain"? My punctured finger's reaction to a pointed stimulus?

The part of Joel's *And So It Goes* that I don't follow is the last line of the stanza: *And so will you soon I suppose*. A lasting marriage is work. I think many people don't agree to working—even though they loudly declare how much they "love." What is "work"? Sometimes, just being present.

Divorce <u>is</u> the most common landmark on today's human coupling landscape.

First the fighting, then the divorce.

I don't share the timbre of Joel's lyrics for his song because he wrote the words from within the feelings that arose during and immediately after a difficult breakup. I assume this. Such a time *is* sad; his lyrics could be a true meditation on the human male-female dynamic.

Like war, marriage *is* hell. Don't listen to anyone who says otherwise. Any honest married man may not use this three-letter word, but he will know what you mean by "hell."

By "honest married man," I mean a man not conducting an affair with a temporarily more-agreeable mistress, and not constantly lying to his wife or playing a false role, and a man who is not away much of the time on business.

The day-in and day-out living with one another and in each other's lives. *This* is real. A happily married man who has been on his half of the couple's rocket for more than one orbit around the familiar star knows *marriage is hell*.

But it's not hell.

Jean-Paul Sartre, the existentialist French philosopher from the mid nineteen-hundreds, said, "Hell is other people." True. A variation on a theme. The hardest thing about living with other people is you can't walk away when they become unreasonable. What is "unreasonable"? Family members, co-workers and spouses. Anyone. An honest couple, in my opinion, has a lot of healed puncture wounds from their contact with the beautiful flower of conjoined marriage. Battle-tested. Worn. The women I have known well have been crazy. By "known," I mean lived with. That's just my opinion. I can't speak for all women because I'm not one—and I haven't known many.

I still make a broad-stroke assumption that *all* women are insane. Not only those who I have known. Every woman is singular and exceptional. Show me a man who thinks otherwise and I'll show you a man who has only admired from afar, or who's never been "honestly" married.

I have my own firsthand experiences and my observations of the marriages around me.

I have always wondered why men lived significantly shorter lives than women. "Men work harder and wear out their bodies sooner," is an easy answer. Men are physically stronger, and yet weaker in a long-term survival sense? Maybe.

The number one activity prescription for a longer life is regular exercise. Do men exercise less than their female counterparts? I doubt it.

I suspect there are many widows out there because they've killed their husbands. Yes.... With relentless drama, insecurity, resentment and other chief ingredients of the gunpowder that make a popular dramatic reality TV show a hit.

Or, have all married men simply committed suicide? Have they sacrificed themselves?

...at least she'll have my insurance money— and she'll be freed from her disappointment in me.

Jokes about the Black Widow abound. Males of some insect species aren't tolerated after their usefulness is past. Is it possible that human males die because they don't have any further purpose in sticking around?

In my estimation, the popular singer-songwriter Billy Joel has written a number of hit songs that were quite bitter complaints about women, even though they sound like nice songs.

"She's Always a Woman" has the beautiful sound of a love song, but it's really pretty scathing in an honest appraisal way. Joel sings this beautiful-sounding melody about the contrary nature of females. I recognize this one, too.

Men and women "get along" like weather "gets along" with itself. Opposing aspects of weather are inextricably tied to one another. It's a singular thing, weather, yet seemingly dichotomized. No lasting "peace" can exist between a beautiful sunny morning and a stormy, lightning-filled, wind-howling rainstorm. Both exist, therefore they are. A tornado and a clear blue sky don't see one another eye to eye; they've got much too much in common—and like a good superhero, you never see them both in the same room at the same time.

Isn't weather something that we see only in passing, like love? Sunny days and stormy days. Such is life, and so...

...it goes.

Another song instilled itself in my head this morning while I was riding mowing. "In Flanders Fields." This tune arrived after the sun had helped the moving wind dry the grass, while the grass was blowing itself out the side of the riding mower in a fine spray instead of in clumps like before.

"In Flanders Fields" has a similar time signature to Joel's "And So It Goes." It sounds the same. Also, there is a similar feeling, although the sentiment is quite different at first glance.

We are the Dead. Short days ago
We lived, felt dawn, saw sunset glow,
Loved and were loved, and now we lie
In Flanders fields.

This war poem was written in 1915 by John McCrae, a Canadian soldier and doctor serving in World War I.

Two years after he penned these words, they were first put to music. The poem is written from the point of view of the dead. The same can be said of Billy Joel's "And So It Goes." The death of a relationship to living—and to once-potential long-term togetherness.

McCrae wrote his poem after presiding over the funeral of a friend and fellow soldier who had died in the Second Battle of Ypres.

Even before his friend's death, it is reported that McCrae was preoccupied by death and how "[death] stands as the transition between the struggle of life and the peace that follows." He was a thoughtful doctor.

Fight with your wife periodically, long enough, and then run across McCrae's words. There will be an appreciation for his point of view even though you have never been to war. In his poem, McCrae seems to tell the living to push on, to continue to live in honor of those whose voices can no longer call to one another in anger or in joy. We must honor those who have died by living on. We married must honor the loss of those who have split apart by continuing on, together.

Joel says to his rapt listeners that relationships are destined to end in "death." He intones with every note of his piano and voice that no lasting relationship is possible.

I know: a war rages, and yesterday, during brief skirmishes and one protracted battle, I didn't know why the other side was attacking. To gain ground? To annihilate? To punish? To destroy without consideration? I found myself marveling, *why all of this destruction?*

Books are written by both sides of this endless war stating what the opponent is after, explaining the other's activities and actions in terms of its own perspective. I should read them, but I never take the time.

"Will men and women ever understand each other," an audience member asked a philosopher during the Q&A after a metaphysical talk at a university lecture.

"No," was the answer, after a pause. "If they're still together by the time they're older, they're just tired." They don't understand each other; they're just tired of fighting. No one has won.

I look forward to such an armistice, and hope it happens *before* my death on the battlefield.

Widows, fairly well set up for money and security, seem mildly appreciative of the memory and accomplishments of their deceased husbands.

My own parents fought strenuously. After almost thirty years beyond my father's death, my mother has a seeming appreciation for him I don't remember her expressing while he was living. They *were*, after all, in the middle of their lives, with children, bills and a family farm. There wasn't time to stop and appreciate one another. It's probably like that for all of us.

Until it's too late, and then we realize that we *never* had the other, but they were there, and so were we. Not anymore.

I would love to be appreciated for my efforts, hopes, dreams, heart and intentions after I am gone.

I imagine I will be misunderstood, underappreciated, misinterpreted, and much less than I would prefer. Some shoeboxes filled with my old black-and-white photo self will be thrown away by people who didn't know me.

When there's an illness or accident, both sides pause and peace reigns at the funeral or in the hospital. Once the soldier is well, if they're well, the fighting may continue. Is life one long battle punctuated by pauses?

Recently, a friend got himself engaged and I don't know why. Maybe I do. He's been living with his fiancée for years and they fight grand, destructive battles that reduce every standing carefully-constructed *bâtiment* to a clean-slate *tabula rasa*.

In the minutes following his engagement, my friend said that they got into another "huge fight." Maybe he is exaggerating. Maybe these frequent battles happen so that peace can happen, so that seeds can be sown in the churned up soil.

Are storms only so that sunny days can be?

Wouldn't it be nice if we could just get along and appreciate sunny days—and each other—and laugh in the rain and hold hands and be fine?

I don't dwell on this—at least not all the time. I have trench foot and shell shock from years in the trenches.

I am a war correspondent dreaming of peace I don't believe exists. Is every war this way? As long as there are two sides there is an agreement to battle.

Sometimes I mow.

Today (the day after mowing), I'm going to drop some packages in the mailbox downtown, and then walk my dog around the village park. It's a beautiful, sunny, cool morning.

And so it goes.

Chapter 30 — Dinosaur Religion

Were *their* congregations under the solemn Banyan trees?

Did *their* pastors make impassioned pleas to each individual listener's charitable instincts to drop donations in the collection basket?

What, *exactly*, did the dinosaurs believe?

Were the dinosaur popes controlling and the Martin Luthers bucking dinosaur systems of thought and control?

Why did dinosaur fortune tellers sense deeply and dinosaur prophets foresee the future? Like the family on a beach before a tsunami, did they notice with a small part of themselves, other smaller, flying dinosaurs leaving in the moments before an asteroid came roiling down from above? Will *we* notice the harbingers of our own ceasing—culturally? Nationally? Personally?

In the tens of millions of years that dinosaurs spread to cover *their* planet with living selves, did they evolve more practically? Pragmatically? Cynically? —than we have managed to become?

Were the dinosaurs Taoists? Did they develop nature religions? Did they practice Yoga and insight meditation or did they chant sutras and pay for a personal mantra? What form were their collection baskets woven into? A ceremonial half-egg? We assume their illiteracy because none of their bibles survived the cataclysm that ushered in their destruction. Have we found one of their fossilized books yet? Their obliging ending was the harbinger of our salvation from marginalized existence and our certain extinction.

Did the dinosaurs tell their children about God? What did their god look like? Isn't this obvious? Did *their* Jesus walk on water or fly with wings?

Is it safe to assume that they had many more Gods? We members of just one speckled species, have thousands. There were thousands of *species* of dinosaur, tens of thousands, even. That's a lot of prayers to go around to a lot of deity forms.

Did dinosaurs' nighttime prayers drown out the sound of the insects? Did dinosaur children close their eyes, bow their heads and hold their forelimbs together? One fateful afternoon, did dinosaur children and adults alike face skyward, forelimbs stretched wide in praise as the heavenly asteroid roiled across the sky on its trajectory to the Yucatán? Do *all* good things come from above?

Were dinosaurs spiritual seekers, unsatisfied by conventional emotional religious dogma sanctioned and sanctified by *their* hierarchical societies? Did they stare at their own reflections in the water? I would have, if I were a dinosaur. Were dinosaurs atheists? Some of them? Secular dinosaurists? Did one of countless millions of dinosaurs, of multiple thousands of species, understand what they were in the grand scheme of things? Did one of them experience a realization of the Truth of existence? Were various dinosaur cults pacifist or activist in nature? Were dinosaurs who committed suicide permitted a dinosaur afterlife or decent burial? Did dinosaur terrorists dream of an after-death reward for *their* actions, including eternal mating with dinosaur virgins?

Were the dinosaurs' souls bigger or better than ours? Did their angels have wings of feathers, or of scales or skin? Is it possible that we are recycled, repurposed and reused dinosaur souls? We're certainly the embodiment, literally, of recycled dinosaurs' bodies. We breathe the air they did, after all.

As the dinosaurs died, the "open" sign on the buffet turned on for all of our warm-blooded ancestors.

What did the dinosaur saints look like in *their* frescos? Were their holy ones depicted with halos? What kinds of religious necklace jewelry did the laity wear? Were *their* rosaries shaped like ours? Did they have stations of the cross in their cathedrals, too? Did they light votive candles for departed loved ones? Did they mention the valley of the shadow of death at graveside funerals? Did they bury their dead, or eat them?

Many discoveries of dinosaur remnants are located where hundreds upon hundreds of dinosaurs of the same and different species were jumbled and tangled together, apparently dying in the same period of time.

Scientists assure us that these individuals were covered with sediment and fossilized. Were they grazing, or running errands, or simply going about their daily business when a terrain-clearing wall of water from a thousand-meter-high tsunami washed them from their homes? Undoubtedly, something happened one day, or in a stretch of days, sixty-five and a half million years ago.

Were these hundreds of dinosaurs all members of a cross-species congregation appealing to deities during their End-of-Days rapture? Were multi-cultural, multi-species mega churches gathering places for members where prophets and soothsayers interpreted the signs of the heavens?

Were dinosaurs as dumb as we believe they were? We think they were dumb, like we think that crocodiles and turtles are dumb. We observe ravens using tools and dolphins having no tools other than cooperation. What is intelligence?

Did dinosaur headstones stand tall and proud for centuries before wearing away finally?

Did deep-throated chanting echo through the valleys with the sound of dinosaur voices joined in unison? Were dinosaurs multi-lingual?

Brain
RECONSTRUCTION HINTS AT DINOSAUR COMMUNICATION

SAN DIEGO — Dinosaur brains may have possessed the capacity for complex vocal communication, a new study hints.

Dinosaurs left behind few clues about their brainpower.
Neuroscientist Erich Jarvis of Duke University and colleagues worked around this problem by studying dinosaurs' living relatives: birds. The team compared the brains of crocodiles, which evolved before dinosaurs, with the brains of birds, which descended from dinosaurs.

Crocodiles and birds have complex brain

regions that help sense other animals' vocalizations, the team reported at the annual Society for Neuroscience meeting. Since birds and crocs both have these regions, dinosaurs probably did too, the scientists suggest.

That finding suggests that dinosaurs such as Tyrannosaurus Rex were capable of processing complex stimuli, such as sounds made by other dinosaurs. As for whether dinosaurs communicated with sound, Jarvis said their study can't say for sure. "But all the structures are there."

In the tens of millions of years that each dinosaur species existed, did they produce something more sophisticated than grunts? Have crocodiles evolved something more than that? Do they need something more? Maybe we don't hear what they're saying. Birds, those living descendants of dinosaurs, do more than grunt. Members of our species find bird noises one of the most beautiful "natural" sounds in our world.

Birds are stupid. They make great-sounding music that I love to listen to while I walk in the forest. Mockingbirds are sublime vocalists. Are these birds just passing on, repeating, and singing the old time religious songs of their forbearers? Singing ancestral music? Mindlessly voicing songs of their former masters? Birds make a lot of sound; but they couldn't be *saying* anything, could they? I don't understand their noises; therefore, I declare that they are meaningless. Isn't *this* the height of stupidity?

All dem animals 'cept us is dumb as shee-it.
Yous rite, dos dinosaurs didn't know nuttin.
N day aint never no such t'ing as dinosaurs,
eeder. I nos wat I no....

Did dinosaurs pray for prosperity and caution their young against unwise excesses? Did dinosaurs *believe* or *know* anything? Did they thank God for their prosperity?

We wise *Homo Sapiens* have whispered to one another that other members of our kind, hailing from other lands with other skin tones and appearances, are unintelligent animals.

Have *you* ever watched a baby dinosaur?

When an individual conscious entity notices the glowing orb in the night sky—or ponders the sun and stars and rainbows and lightning and shooting stars—there is potential curiosity.

Whether wondering, or just staring in wordless awe, religion was our first explanation to ourselves— our first answer to the questions we feel but can't ask about the things we see.

Well, Human God? *What answers do you have?*

Chapter 31 — The Covered Bridge

[trente septembre deux mille treize]

It was cool and fall was coming.

He stepped onto the gravel and locked the rental car with a remote key. It triggered a brief horn blast and the click of automatic door locks.

This always feels good, the man thought. He didn't think these words; he felt something, and acknowledged the feeling. His twelve steps on the way to the first treated road plank crunched lightly on the packed gravel of the cul-de-sac. There was a slight wind. Two six-by-six treated posts stood sentry in front of the covered bridge roadway surface between the gravel turn-around where his rental car was parked and the wooden roadway leading into this 139-year-old covered bridge.

A leaf or two falls when one's gaze rests in any direction, usually accompanying a gust of pleasant morning breeze. When the wind stops, a leaf or two falls then, too. The man's steps echo hollowly on the wooden driving surface of the covered bridge as he nears the open end.

A favorite activity of his is to stand first at one railing, and then on the other side of the wood roadway for just a few seconds each time, taking in the large, open tree-ringed pond on the left with highway sounds coming from I-70 beyond the trees, and then, taking in the right side, which is the swampy and overgrown end of the pond, ringed by vines and thorns, brush, muck, thorn bushes, fallen tree branches and overgrowth lining the water's edge like a balding man's fringe of hair around this rounded end.

A small meandering stream, a mere thread, snakes down from the forest to the pond's end. It is slightly off-center.

This time, the man continued walking sedately past his favorite standing places, into the opening of the red-painted enclosed bridge. It is a structure made of massive squared timbers. Cracks between the floor beams allow one to see the water fifteen feet below in brief reflective flickers.

The covered bridge is 68 feet long and has a gable roof. Its wooden driving surface extends beyond the structure for thirty feet on both ends. It comprises a total constructed length of one hundred and twenty-eight feet.

When he emerged from the other side of the bridge, the man could see that the UFO had landed precisely where he thought it would.

Tripod legs, ending in wide, circular footpads, pressed into the soft, grass-covered topsoil beneath the motionless saucer. The UFO reminded him of an Apollo Lunar Lander model he'd constructed as a boy. This craft rested in a small meadow beyond the bridge's wooden roadway.

Residual heat had scorched the grass beneath the center of the craft. The man looked closely when a hissing sound accompanied the dropping of a panel from the lower curved surface. The panel stopped lowering and extended straight outward to rest softly on the ground in front of his feet.

It was a ramp, six feet wide and metallic. It reminded him of the pull-out ramp from the back of a moving truck, but this was silver-colored, smooth, and looked like something other than aluminum. The saucer was as wide as his house, he guessed—at least thirty-six feet.

A hovercraft!

A train-like shape emerged silently, moving down the ramp like a miniature TGV high-speed French train, complete with trademark sloped front end and smooth, rounded edges. Hovering and silver.

The floating mini-train remained a foot or so above the ramp and glided forward as fast as a slowly-walking person. It had no windows or other features. It transitioned from the ramp over the damp grass in the shade of cottonwood trees along the edge of the pond. It touched nothing. Alongside the man, it paused, silently. Its top was as high as the back of a horse, the man estimated; halfway between his shoulder and waist in height. If it had been on the ground, he could have ridden it like a carousel horse.

He had the urge to jump on it anyway. As soon as this thought occurred to him, he noticed another movement out of the corner of his eye. It was a bipedal creature, silver as well, reminding him of the tin man from *The Wizard of Oz*. It "walked" down the ramp toward him without moving its legs. A yellow-brown leaf landed on top of the motionless mini-train. The man looked down at the fallen leaf. Everything was silent. He couldn't take his attention away from the leaf. He'd seen leaves his whole life, but... now one was resting on an object that he was sure had come from another planet—another galaxy, even.

The silver figure's arms ended in narrow-tipped appendages that moved like an elephant's sensitive trunk or an anteater's tongue. They seemed to probe the very air. Silver.... The figure had no eyes. Was it a walking satellite dish? Where facial features should have been, a wide, convex, round area faced outward. Just an empty salad bowl pointed at him.

The figure stood taller than his own six feet. It had paused at the end of the ramp as though listening, and its head swiveled left and right before pointing again at the man.

Nothing happened for a moment, and then its rounded, flat-bottomed feet rose half a yard into the air. The figure moved forward, toward the bridge, gliding through the air like a parade blimp without wires.

The man glanced back to where the silver figure and mini-train had come from, to the ramp and silently-waiting spacecraft. Suddenly he dodged past the hovering train and ran up the ramp, his feet making no sound. He ran under the UFO in a crouch. The craft's opening was more than tall enough for him to avoid hitting his head but he stayed bent over while he moved to the entrance. He held onto both sides of the smooth metallic opening and leaned in. It was a featureless, empty silver vestibule.

The man didn't notice that the ramp behind him was retracting soundlessly; nor was he surprised when he moved through the entrance of the craft without walking. The panel behind him rose to mesh seamlessly with the silver walls.

Everything... was extremely... *comfortable*.

He walked into the featureless chamber, amazed at how comfortable each step felt. It's the only word he had. *Comfortable*.

The floor was as solid and hard as the walls and ceiling high overhead. Everything was smooth, yet unyielding—and *so, so soft*. He sat at the base of a gently-curving wall.

An overwhelming feeling of peace soaked into his being with every breath. Each expelled lungful carried the weight of his entire life away, lightening him of a lifetime of worries, pressures and fears. With each inhalation, he felt peacefully more solid and contented. For the first time in his life. *Nirvana*.

His thoughts, packaged bundles of words, impressions and reactions, slowed down before finally ceasing. His breathing ceased, as well.

Halfway through a slow, imperceptible exhale, all motion stopped.

His eyes remained open. His face held the expression of equanimity.

*

The bipedal alien placed its prehensile arm on top of what the man had considered a miniature train, triggering a transformation. In moments, the hovering train-shape unrolled into a giant, rectangular, shimmering sail-like sheet of silver. It hovered a constant distance of around a foot above the ground and began to rise at one end like a silent silver tsunami, continuing higher than the gable roof of the bridge. Much, much higher.

One hundred feet, two hundred feet—this seamless sheet of dull, smooth aluminum foil curled up and up, over and down the entire length of the wooden structure—a silver shadow remaining a constant distance from the red-painted outward-leaning gable ends of the covered bridge.

The covering flowed over the timber flooring at both ends of the bridge, keeping its exact distance, stretching from the sentry posts on one end to the beginning of the meadow on the other.

After the silver sheet shadowed every inch of wood construction, it remained still for two minutes. Enough time passed for a couple of dozen more leaves—chestnut, cherry, sycamore and cottonwood—to rest on the silver material that mirrored the contours of the covered bridge.

The radar-dish-faced figure floated over the grass of the meadow until it stepped onto the surface that mirrored the floor surface timbers of the covered bridge. Bipedal alien steps, expressive swinging arms, led up to the covered bridge, where a portal irised in the silver covering. The mute figure stepped into the opening and continued floating above the bare timber roadway inside, through its darkened interior. The silver material irised closed seamlessly behind.

On the gravel turnaround, the man's rental car began to buzz as though its driver were listening to music with a deep bass rumble on the car stereo. A body panel on the car vibrated against the driver's side plastic mud skirting.

In the water beneath the bridge, expanding ripples radiated from the 20 evenly-spaced twelve-by-twelve cross-member-supported stanchions. Bubbles continued to mix with the swirling blackish-brown sediment muddying the water as the entire structure—bridge, pillars, timber roadway and sentry posts—rose slowly.

Pungent fumes from rotting organic matter were released by the action of the stanchions as they drew themselves out of the muck at the bottom of the pond. Half an hour later, three hundred yards up the gravel lane, outside of the Belmont Technical College agricultural annex, a group of students wrinkled their noses upon leaving class. One commented, "The sewer must be backing up."

Twenty minutes before their class ended, higher then the man's parked car, a silver-covered bridge hovered, indifferent to gravity's pull. Drizzling water and black mud plopped below each silently-suspended support pillar. Eleven bats dropped down too, fluttering away from the now too-exposed bridge.

After the bats departed, the silver surface continued flowing under the ends of the covered bridge assemblage, following the contours under the bridge, meeting at the center seamlessly.

The open sides of the completely-encircled bridge began to iris closed. Nothing dropped below the hovering structure any more. A leaf blown from a nearby cottonwood tree landed on the silver-covered roof. The entire form was sealed in dull silver. It hovered twenty feet above the pond where it had stood for 38 winters.

In the meadow beyond the bridge, not far from a double row of planted white birches, the saucer-shaped UFO rose enough to lose contact with the surface of the grass. Its tripod legs retracted, melting into the surface of the craft. From a foot away, a slight humming sound could be heard. No one was there to hear it.

The UFO's outer surface, simultaneous with the covered bridge, became... *not-there*. Unseen, as well as unheard, the spacecraft rose without fanfare. And without interacting with wind currents, it passed through the planet's outer atmosphere within a span of seconds, gaining velocity.

The covered bridge, in tow, and *not-there* to any detection ability possessed by the inhabitants of this planet, followed behind the spacecraft.

None of the hundreds of radar, remote- or direct-sensing devices on the planet, or even in orbit, had detected the arrival of the UFO or its departure with the covered bridge.

Stinking, clouded water in the end of a pond beyond a gravel cul-de-sac stilled and settled. Bubbles still popped on the pond's surface days later, releasing further odors of decomposition.

The man's rental car, a white four-door Dodge Avenger, was towed away, three hours after the bridge's abduction.

Mid-January, after the bridge's disappearance, a graffiti-tagged granite monument was all that remained, standing to the left of the roadway entrance of the former bridge:

> This "Covered Bridge" was once located in Fairfield County, south of Amanda on Clear Creek. It was built in 1875 in the multiple kingpost truss style by Fairfield native and expert covered bridge builder, James W. Buchanan.
>
> The Shaeffer Campbell Bridge was donated to Belmont County in 1975 after being damaged when a farm tractor fell through the floor in 1973. It was dismantled and taken to a county garage in Lloydsville, where it was reassembled and

reconditioned.   This
bridge was placed over
College Pond in 1975.

On the top brochure of a rippled stack of papers inside the Plexiglas-protected literature holder, a caption beneath the sun-faded photograph of the bridge adds:

This 68-foot-long (21 m) wooden bridge sits atop wooden slat-pressured trusses that reach into the muddy bottom of the College Pond. The railings of the approaches to the bridge are designed to mirror railings found on the home of American writer, Mark Twain. The wooden floor of the bridge was built to support loads of wagons and horses, but has not been reinforced for automobile usage, leaving it closed to vehicular traffic but open to pedestrians, such as a cross country event for local high schools every year.

The structure has slanted front supports, allowing the roof to extend further than the sides. The shingles on the roof are laid in a way to allow water to run off without leaking through the small gaps between panels. The sides of the bridge are wooden planks nailed vertically with a small gap between the roof and the top of the side walls. The bridge is normally painted red and is visible from both lanes of Interstate 70, which runs less than 1,000 feet south of the bridge.

On the early fall day that UFO took the bridge, the abducted man's car was examined by two Belmont County Sherriff's deputies responding to incredulous reports from several students who had walked to the bridge after class.

Ten minutes earlier, standing at the edge of the pond, a student half-shouted into his iPhone to the 911 dispatcher.

"Yo, I said the bridge is *gone*!"

The unlit cigarette dangling from his mouth moved when he talked.

Afterword

The real I is beneath action and stillness. It has said nothing.

Each preceding piece featured some aspect of first person, singular. *Everything* is a singular character—be it bridge, questioner, man grilling burgers or salamander.

Acknowledgements

I must thank my wife, Andrée. We share our lives and we help one another with whatever we're working on. In this case, her computer assistance, photography, critical reactions and uncounted other ways are more than a part of this finished work. I am eternally grateful.

Nothing can exist without "help" to make it so. Sheri Rink, positive proofreader *canadienne* of the very first draft of this book, thank you. Your early commentary was an encouragement that I appreciate.

Finally, I want to acknowledge the contribution of the subject matter of *Situations Of I*: namely, my life and everything I see around me. *Thank you*. Without you, this book wouldn't, couldn't, be.

About the Author

From baling hay to newspaper reporter, the author has a skill set derived from employment and self-employment in three countries and five states.

He was raised with a brother and sister in Mid-Michigan by a German Protestant father and an Irish Catholic mother. After an eternal youth spent riding horses, falling out of trees, butchering chickens and hoeing in the garden on their small family farm, Weimer joined the U.S. Army while still a junior in high school in order to have an adventure and to visit his pen-pal, Andrée Lepérou.

He married his pen-pal from Bretagne, France, in 2000. Afterward, they lived in Stuttgart, Germany where Guillaume, their first son, was born. Two years later, they built a skate park in the South of France near Toulouse. In 2004, they were in Howell, Michigan, where Benjamin, their second son, was born. The author and his family currently reside in the northeastern hills of Ohio near Wheeling, West Virginia.

Weimer served a two-year enlistment at Fliegerhorst Kaserne in western central Germany following his father's drowning in Lake Superior. This paternal tragedy turned a natural curiosity about various phenomena in the world into a yearning for the Truth of all things.

*

The author's first published work, *Portrait of a Seeker*, is an unusually-formed catch-all autobiography chronicling a wonderer-turned-seeker of Absolute Truth.

His second publication, *A Handyman's Common Sense Guide to Spiritual Seeking*, was intended as encouragement to those desiring their own ultimate Answer.

Weimer's third published work, *Ben and the Dragon*), began as a story for his then eight-year-old son for Christmas, featuring Ben in an otherworldly adventure with dragons.

Situations Of I is, in the author's words, "Writing I wanted."